SONORA

SONORA

Hannah
Lillith Assadi

Published by
Soho Press, Inc.
853 Broadway
New York, NY 10003

Library of Congress Cataloging-in-Publication Data

Assadi, Hannah Lillith
Sonora / Hannah Lillith Assadi.

ISBN 978-1-61695-792-6
eISBN 978-1-61695-793-3

1. Teenage girls—Fiction. 2. Female friendship—Fiction.
3. Infatuation—Fiction. 4. Sonoran Desert—Fiction.
5. Phoenix (Ariz.)—Fiction. 6. New York (N.Y.)—Fiction.
7. Psychological fiction. I. Title
PS3601.S77   S56 2017   813'.6—dc23
2016038000

Printed in the United States of America

10 9 8 7 6 5 4 3 2 1

For my mother and father, always
& in loving memory, g.g.

And he said unto them, I am an Hebrew; and I fear the LORD, the God of heaven, which hath made the sea and the dry land.

Then were the men exceedingly afraid, and said unto him, Why hast thou done this? For the men knew that he fled from the presence of the LORD, because he had told them.

Then said they unto him, What shall we do unto thee, that the sea may be calm unto us? for the sea wrought, and was tempestuous.

And he said unto them, Take me up, and cast me forth into the sea; so shall the sea be calm unto you: for I know that for my sake this great tempest is upon you.

Nevertheless the men rowed hard to bring it to the land; but they could not: for the sea wrought, and was tempestuous against them.

Wherefore they cried unto the LORD, and said, We beseech thee, O LORD, we beseech thee, let us not perish for this man's life, and lay not upon us innocent blood: for thou, O LORD, hast done as it pleased thee. So they took up Jonah, and cast him forth into the sea: and the sea ceased from her raging. **—Book of Jonah, King James Bible**

CONTENTS

AUGUST

I HAVE ALWAYS MISSED watching the sun fall down into the desert. It is always so slow. There are no windows in the waiting room. The fluorescence blares on despite the romance of the hour. A nurse greets us, my mother and me, and tells us not to look so worried, that my father won't feel a thing.

There are no other families waiting with us. There is no one to distract us. The doctor promises the surgery will help my father walk without pain. My mother is picking at her cuticles. I shuffle the coins in my jacket like prayer beads and make myself automatic cappuccinos to deliver me from the disinfectant, the syrupy trace of fresh death. The television is on mute. We hear the discordant heart monitors of strangers, their parade of breath. We are fleeting visitors, they are here to stay. No one has died yet.

I take my first cigarette break at dusk, and then every

half hour after that. There is a sign that prohibits smoking a hundred feet from the hospital entrance, but I walk farther, all the way to where the grass ends and the dirt of the reservation begins. I meditate on a vague mantra, of touching the earth to soothe the soul. The desert, once dark, is slurred with new lights, traffic on the freeway, sirens rushing on in the distance. I escape the hospital light but cannot escape the swell of memory that assails me only when I am here, back in Sonora. I wonder about the anesthesia, close to death as it brings us, about whether or not our dreams go on when we go under, and if they do, what my father is seeing.

I SEE US IN the dusk beyond, as we once walked in a land wrought for ghosts—the coyotes' silver coats marring the dark. We walked despite their weeping, unrepentant and desolate. It was only at dusk that the land was thronged by spirits, the wind in the brush a moan, a song. My memory of it is folded into one long night, one melodic collapse into the blue-black bigness of the night sky.

From the canal, we returned home, my father and I, saying nothing at all, through a brief and feral silence until streetlight. It was August when we first arrived, the month of monsoons.

The carpet was thick and scratchy and a stained maroon. The blinds never quite closed, so the rooms were always pierced with angled sunlight. Smoke, Turkish coffee, and cat shit pervaded the apartment. We always had a male Siamese blue point, and when one died we got another, and they were all named Sharmut—the Arabic word for whore. When my father wasn't driving a taxi, he sat in the after-school hours, a cigarette in one hand, a glass full of ice and vodka in the other, watching battles roar in deserts on the other side of the planet. My mother worked the night shift at Denny's, the only restaurant in what was once a small town, and as a secretary for a dentist during the day. To relax between shifts, she retreated to the bedroom and watched aerobics tapes, never quite fully following the moves, resting on the floor at the first sign of sweat.

Every day, my father and I walked through the desert to and from the elementary school. In the morning, guiding us silently were Laura and her father. Though we never spoke, it was established that we follow the path they had carved before we ever arrived. Laura's father always wore a sombrero. They never seemed to notice our following them. They never turned around. In stretches, my father yanked me from walking too close to jumping cholla, triggered by even the breeze, resulting in an entire arm or limb smothered in spine. I never paid attention to the threat at every step. I was always watching Laura.

Laura wore sandals every day. Her magenta skirt blew in the brief wind. It was ankle length and tied at her waist with string because it was too big and it was not just that the color was her favorite but the item she would miss forever once she had outgrown it. We all had one. That magenta skirt was always violent beside the dull brown surroundings, but the rest of her, her skin, her hair, was brilliant beneath that sun. She was all caramel, luminous. She walked without fear, as if she were made of the desert vegetation, made of cactus, made of dirt. I yearned to know her even then. Nothing else was of interest on those walks. The sky was always blue, cloudless. Our skin, no matter the month, hot to the touch. Sometimes I became lost in the fancy of a fairy tale tied to the articles of clothing caught in the branches and beneath rocks, a single dirty sock, an abandoned shoe. The desert, so dead, was always littered with our leftovers—evidence of the living.

I do not remember how many months we trailed the path of Laura and her father, but I remember the morning the entrance we had used into the desert was blocked off by orange signs. There were three construction workers sitting with cigarettes in the shade of a paloverde. Laura and her father were nowhere. A police car with its siren lights going pulled up beside us. The officer rolled down his window, asked if we needed assistance. "You know where you are, sir?"

My father shook his head and pulled me close as if my body were a shield. "We used to walk here," he muttered.

A year or so later, the cacti were removed for the scaffolding of the high school Laura and I would attend. Before there were any windows or floors, there was a flagpole. The football field was finished first. The workers slept beneath the bleachers, the only shade that remained. It was an ugly view, all that steel rising up against the mountains. My father said it would never be finished. I hoped that he was right. I was never a girl who yearned to grow up.

Some nights while my mother was at work, my father and I took drives in the taxi he called his *Battlestar Galactica*. The engine softened the coyotes' howls. One of these nights, we drove by way of a dirt road that rose up into the Superstition Mountains. On the drive, one arm out the window with a cigarette, my father spoke of other deserts where he once lived, deserts populated by gazelles, undulating dunes guarding hidden jinn where beyond us only stick-figure saguaro stood. He played the classical station on the radio as the soundtrack for his stories until we passed into the range, where it became too quiet to have music on even in the car.

"There is treasure here, piles and piles of gold," he said when we entered the mountains.

The Arabic moon, a crescent, was a sliver on the horizon. Venus blazed below. My father grew quiet, at last humbled by his present setting, before embarking upon a new story set in the desert in which we found ourselves and featuring the range we soon would become stranded in. He told me of the Lost Dutchman who on his deathbed had given his nurse the secret directions to a hidden gold mine in the Superstitions.

"Maybe we can find it, Ahlam, and when we do, everything will change," he said. I stared out the window, looking into the black range for some glint of gold.

"When you are rich, your past disappears. You get everything you want when you want it," he said. "Everyone wants to know you. Everyone wants to be your friend."

A few minutes later, the engine died. The view we had had of the night sky was now blocked by a veil of mountain. The lights of Phoenix had disappeared miles back.

"Are we lost?" I asked finally, watching my father on the hood of the *Battlestar*, waving for reception on his foot-length mobile phone.

"Go to sleep," he said.

I pretended to sleep as he smoked his Parliaments, finishing one and with each extinguishing bud, beginning another, surrendering only when the dust had risen so thick it covered the stars. My father jumped into the car and closed the windows. Everywhere there was thunder. The sky was torn asunder in purple. And there was the rain, thick on the windshield, thick on the steel of our *Battlestar*.

I know that I hadn't fallen asleep when the sounds of the storm dissolved into a chorus of voices, their screaming emanating from within me instead of without. I know that it was not a dream when I saw Laura. She was just outside our window, dressed in a charcoal-grey cocktail dress. Mascara streamed down her face. Her hair had lost its dark luster, turned ashen. Her body was still a girl's but her face suddenly that of a woman. She was tied upside down from a saguaro cactus, crucified by way of her legs rather than her arms. She began to swing as the wind picked up. The dust rose. She was weeping, her eyes prosecuting, wide. *Soon you will be blind*, I wanted to say. But the wind was so bellowing and the sand so swirling between us, it was difficult to tell which of the two of us needed the warning.

My father shook me, and I came to. He was speaking in Arabic, reading verses of the Quran over my forehead. I was covered in sweat.

"I feel cold," I said.

"It was just a dream," my father said.

Every night we meet the faces of those we love in our dreams. Every night we meet ourselves in the faces of others. Dreams must be love's purest territory. Some dreams dissipate with the morning, some dreams recur. Some dreams appear in broad daylight, some emerge impossibly.

My visions began in the desert and with Laura. Seeing her on that mountain in the middle of the night. In the years that others grew breasts and added inches to their height, I grew fever dreams. My body would suddenly go cold, my head heavy. I felt faint. A chorus of voices converged in me, and then a flash of sight, quick as a dream. In the day or two that followed, my temperature would rise. I'd fall sick. No medicine ever brought me back, only the low sound of my father's words conjured me away from the possession.

With the light of morning, we saw where we were. There were branches tossed into the road. Everything smelled of sage and the smoke of creosote. The sun had fully risen by the time a man in a rusted Chevy pickup drove up and stopped beside us. Without saying hello or good morning, he asked us why we were there. "You know these mountains are haunted," he said. "The Apache guard this place. It's their underworld."

My father squinted against the light. "No, we did not."

The man, strawberry blond with sunburned skin, turned off his ignition. He stepped out of his car, revealing dusty boots, ripped jeans, and a camouflage fatigue button up, to retrieve some jumper cables from the bed of his truck. He wobbled over to us.

My father eyed the gun tucked into the man's hip. He squeezed my hand.

"What's that accent you got?" the man asked my father.

"It's from"—he paused—"the Holy Land."

"I'm Woody," the man said.

"I am Joseph," my father said. "And she . . ." He squeezed my hand tighter. "She is Ariel."

"Nice Christian names," Woody said.

We followed Woody on the dirt road that led out of the Superstitions onto Highway 60.

"Why'd you lie to that man?" I finally asked my father. "Why did you lie about our names?"

"You will understand when you are older. Ariel is pretty. You can use it when you want. Don't ever become attached to your name, Ahlam, or to the place you are from. Just tell people what makes them smile. It's always better to be easily forgotten."

I understood later that the place my father was from had disappeared into a new name. Or an old name. And that it was easier to say that he was from the Holy Land. I understood later that my father came to America and then fled to the desert because he believed that place to be his curse, a mark on his birth he could never run far enough from. That the same place both my parents were from was spoken of often and was the place over which the blood of thousands had been spilled. A place that provoked an endless war that began when my parents were born and still has not ceased. I understood that my mother being from Israel and my father being Palestinian was something that made them feel lonely together, and that was why they never felt at home anywhere except for perhaps, against all odds, with each other.

To me, it was always an underworld, the voices from thousands of years in the past, condemning the present. An underworld where the dead lurked, as it was for the Apache, in those mountains where I saw Laura as a ghost and not as a girl.

I remember little else of our early years in the desert. I remember when there was suddenly a Burger King, a Dairy Queen, a Chevron built in the desert where we had only months earlier walked. I remember the signs for new housing developments, one after the other, advertising larger and larger pools, and three instead of two-car garages. I remember the smell of my dance studio, of the wood and the hairspray and the lipstick and the alternating men and women at the piano as we stood rigid at the bar performing first and second positions. I remember when the high school was finished and that the coyotes disappeared with it. I remember that come dusk, beyond the walls that separated this America from theirs, there where the sun dipped down over the reservation, I saw sea. It was only there that the carcass of saguaro, naked of spines, elegant as piano skeletons, could rest, could rot; there that unbridled horses wild and fast and white as unicorns still reigned.

I found Laura again at a football game the August of my freshman year. I'd never seen a football game. Everyone else was in jeans. My mother made me wear a black lace top, a burgundy chemise beneath it. A dark cherry taffeta skirt. Everyone else had liquor in water bottles. There was a small dance party held at the school after the victory. I danced with a boy to a song about a girl being dead and still haunting the dreams of the singer until he broke away from me. I sat in the bleachers and discreetly sniffed at my shoulder, admiring the faint residue of cologne the boy had sweated onto my skin when Laura sat down next to me. "How's his Axe body spray smell? Is it very special?" She stared on at the crowd before us.

Her voice was deep even then, resonant, and hoarse. I didn't know whether or not to laugh. My hands turned bright red and wet as they had ever since I was a child and nervous.

Laura turned to me. She had amber eyes. They alighted from her deeply tanned face like a beautiful curse. Her hair was streaked magenta. "I'm Laura," she said. She pronounced it the Spanish way, though no one else ever did. We sat there quietly observing the others. Laura hummed a tune dreamily as if I weren't there at all.

"He smelled like shit," I said.

"Fuck, the stupid fireworks have begun," she said, looking up.

The high school was hailed as the most beautiful school in the valley with its floor-to-ceiling windows and elegant outdoor walkways, its Greek columns mixed with modern architecture. There was a public library housed in its interior. I smelled no chalk, no glue, no rubber cement, no sunscreen. No children had ever been there. Everything was too new. The high school was erected on Yavapai land. This was normal. The entire city was erected on someone else's land. My father told me to be vigilant. "The Navajo won't touch Anasazi ruins because of the jinn that go inside of the coyotes."

"It's the Hohokam that were here," my mother corrected him.

"They are brothers, same people," he said.

As we passed through the gates of the school each morning, my father asked, "Do you remember when there was nothing here, when it was dark, quiet?"

"It's still empty and quiet and dead," my mother said.

The first week of school, one of the surveillance cameras caught the fluorescent lights flashing on and off through the halls long after all the janitors had left. Over the course of the next four years, this would happen sporadically both when school was in session and when it was not. The administrators blamed the recurrence on the monsoons, even when it was not monsoon season.

———

AS WE AWAIT MY father's waking, I smoke outside and stand apart from the desert as the darkness falls. Every movement in the brush sends me leaping back onto the pavement. The desert scares me because it is empty, always shuddering, condemning me to memory.

My mother calls, asks where I am. She begs me to come back inside, to smoke less. She says we need to comfort each other. The reservation, once empty and vast, now has three casinos with trailing LED lights as facades. The facades broadcast the falling leaves of elsewhere. They are the tallest buildings in the valley but are Legos beside the mountains. Their parking lots are full. Before them stand new office buildings, new malls, a structure made to resemble a flying saucer, a butterfly museum, another Walmart. I make out two stars.

———

IN HIGH SCHOOL, I learned to dress my eyes with thick kohl. I learned to smoke when Laura told me that tobacco was used as a shroud for those who walked in the underworld. She said that the indigenous people of this land knew how to use it, but the white man destroyed it. I used too many bobby pins to tie up my too-long hair. All of these things are still with me: eyeliner, bobby pins, tobacco. With the years, we become even more ourselves and call this change.

I wore black or charcoal grey, tones of rain and the night sky. Laura had outgrown her magenta skirt, but she'd found others equally bright. In bad moods, she wore grey. Never black. She drew skulls on her palms in colored pens, and I weekly helped her apply a temporary tattoo of a coyote to her upper arm. "My spirit animal," she said when I first peeled back the paper from her skin.

She wore rings on every finger—turquoise, lapis, fake rubies. Her nail polish was always half picked off, tiny islands of color. Only one nail was not chewed off, preserved for the guitar. She wore spider web tights in the summer. In winter, she wore coyote fur. The walls of her room were covered in old newspaper clippings, sightings of the mythological La Llorona and other supernatural phenomena in various ghost towns throughout the desert. She had a cabinet devoted to stolen goods from the mall: underwear, blush, perfume, dream catchers. Laura always wore a choker made of rope with a dangling cross and locket. In her upper half, she was a dancer, her neck long and elegant, her chest puffed out prettily. But her lower half gravitated to earth, full hipped, her feet flat and awkward as any bird. I did not recognize her as pretty as a child. It was only when we were older that her face became unavoidable, handsome and primal.

At school, Laura and I were sometimes called goths, sometimes gross lesbians, sometimes just witches or freaks. For lunch, we sat together beside a large window that looked out onto the desert. On the way home, we took the school bus. A group of boys sat in the back, railing on the girls in the front seats. Among them was the son of a popular English teacher who went by the nickname Sweet'N Low and liked to ask girls crude questions about various sexual acts. We had escaped his attention for weeks until the day he sat down in an empty seat behind me and said, "Hey, goth girl, tell us what a blow job is."

I looked to Laura for help, but she was humming, staring out the window. He waited a moment and then stood, took a bow, and yelled, "Ladies and gentleman, I present you with the blow job girl." This was followed by a chorus from the back of the bus: *Blow job girl, blow job girl.* Laura lunged at him and tore at his face with her strumming nail.

"What the hell?" Sweet'N Low looked as if he was going to cry. She had barely drawn blood. "You're fucking crazy."

"I dare you to tell on me," she said, then resumed her humming trance at the window.

I got off the bus at Laura's stop, one stop earlier than my own. Laura walked ahead of me and toward the entrance of the reservation.

"You live here?" I asked.

"My mother did," she said. "But my father's white, so we don't."

"You think he'll tell the bus driver?"

She shook her head and looked darkly toward the bus as it pulled away.

"Try not to walk on the cracks," she said. "See how I'm doing."

"Why?"

"That's where ghosts live."

"I'm the other way," I said and nodded in the direction of my apartment complex.

"See you tomorrow, blow job girl," she said and flicked my arm.

The popular kids all sat in the center of the lunch hall on showcase. The rest of us found corners to hide in. Trevor sat in the center of the center, flanked by the cheerleaders on one side and the football team on the other. Trevor lived in my apartment complex. Because his parents were waiting for their mansion to be finished, he explained to me.

At the apartment complex, Trevor and I saw each other at the pool. The water was green from lack of maintenance and ridden with paloverde branches. Trevor would clasp his hands over my mouth, dunk me in, hold me there until I kicked and fought to come up. Some afternoons, he would lodge himself on top of me on the lounge chairs, straddling me, his daily white shirt still wet from the pool, his fingers smelling of sweat and dust. Some afternoons he would rock back and forth on my lower belly. Despite my cries for him to get off, an unwelcome purring took me. I'd never been touched.

But Trevor did not speak to me at school. He pretended not to know me. Trevor was a punter on the team at our high school. He drank beer. He was a star.

One night after a football game, Laura led me to a party where Trevor was. When we approached the keg, Trevor asked loudly who invited the freaks. I flushed. Laura walked toward him and grabbed a fistful of his hair and pulled.

"Who let this Mexican trash in here?" Trevor screamed.

"Assholes," she cried as we ran outside.

We walked through the wash to the edge of the reservation in silence. Laura sat down on a stone and handed me a beer she had stolen from the party. "Wanna dance?" she asked.

"I hate people," I said.

Beneath the moon, she faux-waltzed before me. "Just imagine there are thousands of couples, music playing. The ocean is just off in the distance. Don't you like long sunset walks on the beach?"

I laughed from the one beer it took me to be drunk. "Have another?" I shook the can.

"I have this," she said and pulled out a water bottle that smelled more like rubbing alcohol than spirits. Laura began to dance awkwardly again, her hair spinning more prettily than her body. I gurgled the drink and spit it into the rocks. She fell toward me, dizzy.

"Wanna see something weird?" Laura lifted her shirt up, revealing a lavender bra that was too large for her small breasts. Her chest was scarred faintly red in the pattern of tree veins. "I was struck by lightning as a child," she said. "For most people, the scar disappears after a few days or a month. But mine never faded."

"It's sort of pretty," I said, wishing I had some mark to show of my own.

"But what if it's some sort of curse? Or, like, a map to a constellation where there are aliens?"

"Or a map to the gold in the Superstitions," I said.

"Yeah, right. There's no gold there, just ghosts." She kneeled down and put her finger to a cactus needle. The blood bubbled like ink and trailed off her hand into the dirt. "Come here," she said. Before I knew it, she had taken my finger to a spine then pressed it into hers. "Now you have a scar too."

"Hardly," I said.

"With this prick, we are blood sisters. Together forever."

I HAVE ALWAYS LOVED those with beautiful scars. My father was born with a mark beneath his calf he claims is the exact shape of his homeland. I wonder if the doctors ever notice, if they wonder at a body, its marks of particularity, its pinpricks of love, of drunken stumble, of bruise. Or if in their haste to save our lives, it is only our blood pressure, our liver function, our heart rate that concern them. If an alien beheld the earth and saw us scrambling for the rush-hour train, pumping gas at the local station, slowed in the highway traffic, our bombs fireworking the sky, they might think we are the scars. We are the wounds. This is why aliens always appear in the desert. It is empty. It is clean.

I SNUCK OUT WITH Laura in the night. We could not drive, so we got picked up. We snuck under gates and climbed over walls. We walked through the desert by night. Laura taught me to suck on pennies if drunk and caught by cops. Laura instructed me about the various ways in which I could bring myself to orgasm, her favorite being lying beneath a bath faucet. She told me of the ointments witches rubbed onto their broomsticks, shoving the ends far into themselves. "Witches never really flew, Ahlam. They were just getting off."

The image of us that remains forever is always in a stranger's car, the windows down, Laura singing, my hands wet with fear. Like the night Laura was singing along to a song called "Blue American." The boy driving was coming down off meth. Dylan would have been in the passenger seat.

I'd never seen what it meant to come down until I saw the boy, his blond hair streaked blue, collapse into maniacal tears at what he called the beauty of Jesus and the desert in the middle of the night and crystal. And crystal.

Laura squeezed my hand and rolled down the window to smoke a cigarette. "Don't be so serious," she said. "No one's going to die. Have a little fun."

I had asked the boy who wept what it felt like, crystal meth, the prettiest name for a drug beside heroin. Crystalline methamphetamine. His head fell back. He closed his eyes, then opened them. "Come on, you know . . . you're just high as fuck." Then in a dramatic whisper: "Everything goes silent like a midnight of the mind."

My father punished me as a child with what he called the "silence jail." When I got into trouble or threw a tantrum, he would tell me to go into my room and "practice silence." When an hour of silence had passed, he would come into my room, sit down on my bed and tell me the same story he'd told me the last time. When his family left Palestine, he was smuggled out in the night in his mother's arms at four days old. "Silence is my first memory," he would say. "My mother had her hand over my mouth to muffle my cries. What baby is not allowed to cry at birth? That is silence. That is real silence. Do you see how lucky you are? A child in America. No war. Just peace and prosperity and a beautiful, big desert to play in."

My mother never spoke of home, never spoke of missing it. My mother never remembered her dreams. My mother only ever missed New York. My mother could never stand silence.

⤙⤚⤙⤚⤙

MY MOTHER IS LICKING an empty M&Ms bag. She does this when she is nervous—licks her empty plate or an empty package of candy or chips. The television murmurs on in the waiting room. A sitcom plays. A family is driving somewhere, the children roll their eyes, the father honks at a stoplight. Their house is large. Its yard has a tree. They have a dog. They have God. I hold my mother's shoulder, and we watch the scenes unfold. "Do you think you'll ever have a child?" she asks me.

"It's not something I'm considering at the moment," I say.

"Well, you don't want to get too old."

I walk toward the television and turn the volume up. "I'm twenty-three."

"You are just like your father." She begins to cough, a dry, achy cough she's had for years. "I was married at your age," she says hoarsely. "Don't worry about the cough. Everyone has it here. Valley fever."

"You know, they're planning to round up all the wild horses," I say. "Did you hear about that? That they are going to round up all the wild horses on the reservation and otherwise dispose of them?"

"So they'll send them somewhere else?"

"'Otherwise dispose of' means kill them, Mom."

"Don't be morbid," she says.

"But it's the truth," I say.

THERE WAS A GAME my parents played as I grew up. My father would blast the news even through dinner. He would only turn it off when the local newscasters came on to broadcast game scores, the rising temperature throughout the week, puppy shows, and celebrity sightings. He would also turn it off when the president spoke. But if there was news from Iraq, Kuwait, Israel, or Palestine, there would be no reprieve.

My mother would take the remote to mute it, pleading he wait until we were finished with dinner. My father would stand, get a glass of water, and put the volume back up. My mother would talk to me about my homework, my dance class, her voice rising in volume to compete with whatever reporter was on the screen. My father cursed in Arabic in response to the same reporter delivering his requisite dose of tragedy.

My mother would rise from her seat, collect the dishes,

our meals half eaten, and rinse the plates loudly at the sink. Midway through the clatter, my father would say, "But I wasn't finished."

One morning, Trevor was on the news. He was missing. My father flipped the television off. "Aren't there more important things in the world to report?"

"I've seen that boy around," my mother said and turned it back on.

"These fucking Americans," my father said and muted the volume.

It remained muted through scenes of floodlights focused on the desert in the area they believed Trevor had wandered into. Floodlights combing up and down the hills, illuminating only brush and saguaro and emptiness, hovering for a moment, hoping for leg or arm or dash of human hair, only to find the movement to be wind in a paloverde branch.

When the principal announced the news about Trevor, my blood turned electric. I rushed from class into the bathroom. I sat on the toilet seat and shut my eyes. My hands were damp. My veins wormed beneath my skin. Something was rocking over me. My belly down to my groin, warm. I smelled rust. The voices were taking over. And then I was at the canal. There was no high school. We were swimming in it. The water was clear as a pool. The bodies intermingled with fish and sunken cacti. Trevor made waves. Kids were running between the paloverde. Laura appeared from the brush. I pulled myself out of the water to greet her.

The sky turned grey and snow began to fall. The trees covered as if by fleece. The water froze over. Everyone was still as statues. Except for Laura and me, it was a sudden graveyard. The sky fell to dusk. Laura tiptoed onto the icy canal. I tried to shout but could not speak, and so I knelt down on the banks with my head tilted up to swallow the snow just as the ice shattered slowly and as helplessly as glass. When I looked at Laura again, she was knocking heavily upon the frozen surface as if upon a door.

For the first time, there was blood in my underwear. I went home from school early.

Laura called when I did not return the next day. "They found him," she said.

"Oh?" I said hopefully.

"Dead. The whole school is wearing black just like you, A."

"Oh my God, Laura."

"You better come back before they think you did it."

Trevor was the first to die. He wandered away from the party hours after Laura and I had left. Wandered miles into the desert much farther than the path she and I had taken home. It took four days for a policeman on horseback to follow a trail of blood that led to a lot of abandoned, half-constructed homes.

There he found Trevor bled to death, the honey brown of his skin pale, his lips blue as his eyes. Lacerations ran the length of his arm. He was missing his clothing and his shoes. The news blamed the coyotes.

There was never further investigation. We heard that his mother was seeking out psychics and mediums. Laura and I saw her sometimes sitting at the newly opened Starbucks deep in conversation with women, examining tarot cards, her face red with tears. Trevor's parents moved out of the apartment complex a week after his death. Their mansion must have been complete. Rumors circulated that the women told his mother Trevor was wandering still, that he had something to say.

When we arrived, before the high school was built, before the coyotes disappeared, we ate dinner on the porch of our apartment and watched the sunset splashing crimson and lavender across the brush. A hush came over the desert at that hour. Once it was dark, the hush would be corrupted by howling. The coyotes were hungry. My father bought two extra steaks and left them raw in plastic bags. It was a secret we kept from my mother. The nights she was at work, I held his hand and followed him out of the apartment complex and into the desert. We walked by moonlight or flashlight up until we reached the canal. Here the dirt path stopped. The desert was everywhere, empty but for the coyotes. The bag dripped in my hands, and the pink blood left them sticky, smelling of iron and sweat. "Do not be afraid. They will not bite. They are scared more than us," my father said.

Every night we came, carefully navigating the cactus, listening to the coyotes whisper against the brush, their silver coats marring the dark. Every night they came closer to us, until at last we could stand right before them, their sweaty noses wetting our hands. "You give back to your home so that it doesn't come for you. You look it eye to eye," my father said.

Every night we came until the night the coyotes gathered around us, only to suddenly scatter. We looked up, and there was a blur of light crashing toward us. For an instant the sky turned brighter than morning. My father picked me up and ran for home.

FEBRUARY

THE LAND IS OLD. The land is rumored to be full of vortices and voids, of paths into the underworld, and landmarks of landings from other worlds. We settled in by renaming the mountains. My father chose a mountain for me. It is known to everyone else as Fire Rock after its reddish hue. The mountain has jagged drops between rising peaks. From the hospital, I spot its silhouette as the last light escapes the valley, and trace the difficulty of its lines and wonder at my father for choosing such a broken mountain to call by my name.

***

DYLAN ARRIVED IN OUR lives with the Phoenix Lights. The Lights were the lights everyone saw, and they appeared over the Superstitions in the east, the home of the Apache underworld, and disappeared over the Estrella Mountains. The week we met him, I remember that my mother had a migraine every day. She remained on the couch in the dark while my father juiced lemons on her temples and forehead. He read the Quran over her. She begged him for migraine medicine. "But it's poison, pure poison," he said. "Your migraines are a spiritual problem."

The night of the Lights, my father's taxi shift did not end until four in the morning, but by eleven o'clock, he was home. He told us to get in the car. It reeked of marijuana. My mother complained of the smell, said her headache would surely return. My father said she should try a joint herself and then drifted into Arabic. My father vanished from his own sentences. He muttered beneath his breath. He spoke to his hands as if to ghosts.

My mother opened the windows to freshen the air. It was winter. It was dry and cold inside the bones.

"You know," my father said, "I've survived a lot. I've seen ghosts, angels. Gabriel once spoke to me while waiting for the subway. I almost drowned in the sea. I've seen a lot, but never something like this."

We parked at an overlook near my mountain. In the distance, we saw Camelback Mountain, South Mountain, the thick orange pollution over Phoenix, one or two stars. The valley was always dead after ten at night, but this night we stood with hundreds of others. People had telescopes. It was an event, this longing stretched toward the night.

"I chased it to the end. It disappeared. Huge lights, ruby lights. A triangular ship. A cluster of stars almost, but moving like the sky falling. It rose up over the Superstitions and then just covered the city, covered the sky. Everything disappeared. Then the lights turned blue. Yes blue," my father said.

I saw only Venus, burning white on the horizon. "Guess they just vanished, then?"

"You see, Yusef," my mother said.

"Thousands of people saw it, Rachel," he insisted.

"I'm not feeling well. Can't we just go home?"

"I thought you didn't have pain in the dark," he said.

My father went looking every night after that. Once his taxi shift had finished, he would drive in circles on the outskirts of town, listening to the radio, looking up. Sometimes he asked if I wanted to skip ballet and join him. "Don't you remember what happened to us and the coyotes? Don't you want to find out where that light came from?"

"It was a meteor!" I said.

"How can you be my daughter and really believe that?"

Dance lessons lasted until nine or ten in the evening. Sometimes I would eat dinner, sometimes I would not. My mother prepared steamed broccoli and lean fish for me. My father insisted I eat red meat. "You'll lose your brain without food," he said. A meal to him without beef was starvation.

I threw up at least one meal per day. Laura had taught me

that with your middle finger it always works the first time. In the dressing room before rehearsals and performances, the smell of hairspray on everything, I watched the other girls undress with ease. They chatted in the nude as they applied their blush and their red lipstick. Most were petite, hairless. They were weightless, they could fly.

The first herald of Dylan for Laura was in Mexico. Once a month, she and her father would travel three hours south so he could build new beachfront houses for rich Americans and they could meet their psychic. The psychic only did her consultations on the beach, her clients huddled around her, and only at dusk or dawn. These were the hours, Laura explained to me, that the door to the afterlife was ajar.

Returning from Mexico, Laura's hair lightened, aflame against her skin, she would don sombreros. She carried with her the cheap guitars she'd bought on the beach and strummed them, walking the great halls between classes, not noticing the glances or the snickers, not caring. Those days she walked with the full grace of a dancer, her footprint soft. It was what the ocean did to her, left her floating in its wake. She didn't wash her hair for at least a week after leaving the sea.

We met in the wash beyond the bleachers of our school to smoke after third period. Laura gave the psychic a name, Maria, and said Maria had told her something interesting at last that didn't have to do with her father's business or her mother's messages from the land of the dead.

"First, Maria told me my dark friend and I are about to enter an era of true darkness. Also that a visitor is coming to us and that we should be careful," she whispered, though we were alone.

"And I'm your 'dark' friend?" I asked.

"Then she told me that it is my Indian blood mixed with my Irish that makes me so dangerous. That I'm a witch like my mother, but I don't understand my power yet. That my mother was always an outcast and that I take after her. She said I have vision, that my dark friend has vision too. She said yours travels in dreams. She said we found each other for a reason, you and I. Then right after that, we were driving home, and those aliens appeared."

"She said I have vision?" I asked.

"Did you see the Lights?" she asked. I shook my head. Laura exhaled her cigarette dramatically and extinguished it on the heel of one of her cowboy boots. "It looked like a ship. And the sound it made was like wind, like rushing wind. The surface was like waves. There were seven lights, and I swear they were in the pattern of the Pleiades. They were blue."

"On the news, they said they were red."

"Blue. I swear." She nodded solemnly and clutched her locket.

"What's in there anyway?" I asked.

"My mother's ashes." She pulled at the roots of her hair at her forehead as if trying to make it grow over her face. It was a tic she had. "Library?"

"I'm done with my homework."

"I want to check out a book about how to do a séance."

I looked at Laura, her hair streaked magenta, her sombrero slipped fully from her small head, her eyeliner bleeding, smudged even on her cheeks, and wondered at how many lives before this life we might have known together.

It was in the library that we found him. Dylan was wearing a bow tie and a vest, but his dress shirt was cut off above his elbows. His jeans were splattered with paint. He was much older than us, but his cheeks were puffy as a child's. On the table before him was a pocket watch. On his left arm, there was a trail of rose-hued burn wounds, some outlined in ink. I'd never seen anyone like him, so boldly himself, the jumble of centuries in his attire.

He looked up from what he was reading and stared into the back of a shelf as if he were peering out over a ship or promontory, looking for sea life and icebergs to rise up from the ocean. Encountering him there was like hearing a rattlesnake rustle in the bougainvillea. There was always so little warning.

"Who is that?" Laura whispered.

"Who cares?" I said.

"It's him," she said. I pulled her arm to leave, nodding toward the exit, though I wanted her to tug back, resist me. I always did. "It's him," she repeated.

"It's some old homeless guy, Laura."

"He's our fate." Laura was already moving toward his table. She walked just past him, breezing his shoulder with her bag, begging him to look up and notice her, but he didn't. She turned, confused, and opened a book from the medical shelf, pretending to intently read. She wouldn't look up at me, though I was mouthing, *Let's go, let's go*. Finally she gave it up and dropped the book on the table where he was sitting.

"Oops," she said loudly. Dylan remained intent on his reading but smiled at the pages, amused.

"Hi," Laura said. "Do you go here?"

"The school, no," he said. "I don't go to school anymore."

"I figured. I'm Laura." Dylan nodded his head, licked his finger to turn a page. "And she's Ahlam."

"Does she know how to speak?" Dylan peered toward me. His eyes were light green but opaque as if covered in tinted glass.

"What are you reading?" Laura asked.

"Stuff on alchemy."

"Why alchemy?"

"It's one of the four magical suites," he said.

"Why are you studying magic?" I asked.

"She speaks," he said. "Why do you go to high school?" The bell rang.

"Laura, we gotta get to class," I said.

"You go ahead."

That night, my parents had a fight. The television was on in their bedroom. I put my headphones on and could still hear the news. There had been a suicide bomb, houses demolished. There had been talks, and the collapse of talks. "Incredible, these fucking Americans show the one Israeli dead and not the hundreds of children they've killed," my father shouted.

"Are you blaming me?" my mother shouted back. "Can't you have any pity? I have a migraine."

"Why do you always have to play the victim?" he asked and slammed the door. I watched him get into his taxi and idle in the parking lot. Sometimes he just did that, sat in his car for an hour with the radio on. But that night he sped out and into the street. My parents always fought when the news turned bad. They fought about grocery receipts, phone bills, the rent. But they never spoke of divorce. If they separated, they would have betrayed the thing that estranged them, the thing that made them special, what made their unhappiness holy. What made our not having any money, the fact that my mother got no inheritance from her parents except a single set of china, exceptional. At least they were rebels in a world that, with age, always sells out.

I heard my mother shut off the television and begin to cry.

There was a knock on my window. I flipped open the blinds.

"Hey," Laura said.

"Hey."

"Come on. Dylan's waiting."

Dylan drove a Chevy pickup from the 1970s. One of the windows had been shattered, the fender hung from the frame of the car, and a side-view mirror was missing. The floor was filled with cigarette butts and empty beer cans. I squeezed in beside Laura.

"Where to?" Dylan asked.

"Wherever," Laura said.

We drove in silence until Dylan put a cassette in the deck.

"Are you serious? Frank Sinatra?" I said.

"It's classic, Ahlam." Laura rolled her eyes at me and elongated my name. She hated Sinatra.

Dylan was singing, paying us no attention. Then he released his hands from the wheel. "Know how to drive?" he asked. "Need to roll a smoke."

"Fuck," I said. Laura began to steer. I put my hand on the wheel with her and began to shake. The voices converged from nothing at all. I heard my parents' argument all over again. The car was vibrating, we'd lose control of it, it could go in any direction, we'd go off the road, hit a saguaro. I saw the saguaro right before us, entering the windshield. I braced. The winter lashed at me through the shattered window.

I saw myself in the night beyond. I was crouching at the base of an ash-covered mountain. In the distance, fireworks shot up and burst apart over them. There was a boy walking out into the night, gun in hand. His hair was so white it could have been blue. He was vaguely familiar to me, though I could not see his face. Laura and I were on either side of him. Another firework shot up over us, and the boy collapsed, dead.

"Are you okay?" Laura touched my hand, bringing me back

to the car. Dylan was steering now, singing along to "New York, New York."

"Can we turn the heat on?" I asked.

"Doesn't work," Dylan said.

It was dark by the time we parked beside a small hill. I splashed water on my face from a half-functioning fountain. I shadowed Dylan closely as he and Laura trudged up and up.

They kept walking. On the hill there was a swing set and a slide, set on a rubber tarp atop rocks and snake holes. Below us lay a lot of half-constructed homes. Dylan sat on one of the swings and pulled out a flask from his jacket pocket.

"What's in it?" Laura asked.

"Bourbon," he said.

I took a sip and choked. Laura snatched it from me and held it over her mouth. "You shoot it directly back into your throat."

We beheld the entire valley. The smog, the dark etches of mountain in the distance, the communication towers flashing red over South Mountain, the planes dipping low into Sky Harbor Airport, and just beyond where the city ended, the Sierra Estrella.

"You see that mountain range over there?" Laura said. "It's called the Gateway to the Stars."

Dylan rolled a cigarette, his two pinky fingers delicately pointing upward as he licked the paper and sealed it.

"Four kids disappeared there the night of the Lights. They were off-roading. And that's exactly where the

Lights disappeared. Right in those mountains." Laura's face was animated, and she was speaking in a higher pitch than usual. "No one has found them."

"What if they just got drunk and killed themselves like everyone else?" I asked.

"Did they ever find their car?" Dylan asked.

"Maybe the aliens took it with them. Or maybe *you* are an alien. Just appearing out of nowhere," Laura said. "Maybe you killed them and used their body parts to make yourself look human."

"Stop that," Dylan said and put out his cigarette. His face changed so completely from the one singing Sinatra. He looked out over the mountain as he had in the library, peering for something in the distance, in the past. Laura flushed and squeezed my hand.

"Let's go swing?" I said.

"I'll tell you a story. This was back in New York." Dylan paused and began to roll another cigarette.

"You never said you came from New York," I said.

"You never asked," he said. "Well, I had these birds, and before I began, you know, traveling like I am now, I knew I had to get rid of them, but I didn't just want to leave them in another cage."

"You smoke a lot," Laura said.

"This one's for you. Maybe it will help you shut up when people are talking," Dylan said. Laura clapped both hands over her mouth jokingly but her eyes were wet.

"Anyways, I had to get rid of them because I was leaving. So I drove out of the city a bit with them and parked beside some woods. I sat the cage on the hood of my car and then opened it." He lit the cigarette for Laura and pinched her cheek. She pushed his shoulder and stood up as if to run away.

"And for the longest time they just stayed in the cage. The father would fly up a bit from his perch and peek his head out for a second, then fly back down. And then one of the little ones would do the same, but basically they all just sat there chirping a little, confused. Finally, I shook the cage a bit, screaming, like, 'Get the fuck out!' Finally one flew out, but he just flew to the roof of the car. Then one by one, they followed. And then one went to the nearest branch, and the others followed. Until they were gone."

"They were finally free," Laura said, stilled in her attempted escape.

"Not free. Dead. Dead in a matter of minutes. No way they'd survive the wild," Dylan said. "But at least they got to fly."

The three of us lay back with our hair in the red mountain dust. I felt as if I was suddenly older. Older in one night. As if by being in proximity to Dylan, I knew things about freedom and death, drinking beers while driving, rolling cigarettes between sips of bourbon, the subway and the woods and the buildings and the parties he must have gone to in New York and sex. I felt I knew even about sex. We had something no one else did in the valley. We were special. We'd found Dylan.

A grey sliver darted through the paloverde. Dylan jerked up and onto his knees.

"Just a coyote," I said.

"That was not a coyote. That was something walking straight up. Looked like a girl, a woman. She was limping. Come on, we gotta get back to the car."

"It was a skinwalker," Laura said. "But only you saw it."

"What the fuck does that mean?" he said.

"It's a ghost that takes the shape of an animal. They only come after certain people and not others," she said quietly.

As we drove back onto Shea Boulevard in the predawn streets, Sinatra playing, the winter with us through the broken window, Dylan rolled another cigarette and released the wheel for Laura, who steered us without fear or hesitation while I sat in the back watching the darkness depart.

Coyotes stayed out of the roads, but when injured, they lost their sense of place. They limped slowly across the dark roads where no lights were, forgetting that the feel of asphalt on their paws meant that, in mere moments, a car would be speeding toward them from around the bend at ninety miles per hour. When the Lights passed over our desert, the coyotes returned to the banks of the canal, ever briefly, howling toward the night as if returning its call.

When I got home from the drive with Dylan, I saw a limping coyote in the parking lot. I feared the animal was the one Dylan had seen, a ghost returned to warn me.

The month the Lights passed over the desert and took four boys with them, there was a slew of suicides at our school. The boys that went missing in the Sierra Estrella appeared only once on the news, and in the months that passed were forgotten in the onslaught of homemade videos and photos of the Lights themselves, appearing always red and orange and never blue. The case of the missing boys was eventually closed, though no evidence of their remains or their car had ever been found.

Four years later, a bear attacked a campsite two hundred miles south of the Sierra Estella Mountains. That same bear was cited as the culprit for the boys' disappearance and death.

The year of the Lights, the suicide rate in Arizona surged three times higher than the national rate. The Lights appeared to my father and Laura and to thousands of others rising up from the east over the Superstition Mountains, disappearing into the Estrella Mountains. But they never returned for me.

The first suicide at our school, Thomas, dove into his backyard pool just as the midnight tarp was closing. He was captain of the swim team but had just been defeated at the state competitions.

The second, Brad, whom no one seemed to know or

remember, hung himself from a tree on the now shut-down elementary school playground. On the grass below him there was an empty bottle of Georgy vodka. And in his pocket, there was a note warning that the Lights were a sign, but he never said of what.

On the school bus, Sweet'N Low stood up and performed reenactments of the two deaths, whining in a girl's voice about not being able to swim like a man or about giving blow jobs to aliens. I shared my headphones with Laura, and we put the volume up.

One morning that suicidal February, I missed the bus so my father dropped me off at school. When I exited the car, he rolled down the window and called my name. "Three things I must say to you. One, you are a beautiful dancer, but the piano will remain with you longer. Two, don't fall in love or let anyone's life become more important than your own."

"Why?" I asked.

"Some women I loved, some women I left, I left in a bad way. I left because I had to leave. Maybe you have a brother somewhere," he said. "I don't know. Maybe worse things. If my sins come back to me through you, I won't be able to breathe. That's history, Ahlam. It's cyclical. Like a curse. Think about what happened to the Jews for decades, then think about the Palestinians. Find someone who loves you more than you love them."

"Dad, I'm late," I said.

"The third thing is that no one leaves a place for a good reason. They leave because they are fleeing from something or because they are being forced to leave. Remember what I am telling you."

He turned the radio up after that and sped away. I heard the fading report that another bomb had exploded in Jerusalem.

My father never quit his search for Lights in the sky to take him elsewhere, as if the Lights might be a time machine, a way to pace backward through the snowbanks of time. My mother got a new job as an office secretary. In the early evenings, she played tennis. At night, while my father was out searching, my mother sat before the muted television, a movie from the fifties playing, the bashful scenes reflecting in the darkened windows that kept the desert out of our house, a bottle of wine emptied, one glass left a quarter full. I tried to wake her when I returned from dance class. She'd call me by my father's name. I shook her again, tell her she had fallen asleep, that it was time to go to bed. It was never lonely when we all three were together. It was only lonely when it was just two. Two is the loneliest number. One can house a crowd.

THE DOCTOR RETRIEVES US in the waiting room. My mother coughs in her sleep. The sitcom has ended. There are only the news and commercials, bombs and psychiatric drugs and airplane crashes and celebrity divorces. I shake my mother. She calls me by my father's name. "It's time," I say. "He's awake."

The lights are off. My father's eyelids shake. His voice is different. His accent is thick. He speaks as if he's drunk. "It was all ocean," he says, and then he closes his eyes again.

I beg my mother to go home and get some rest. I tell her I'll stay. She says she'll come back in one hour. When she returns, we will switch. I fall asleep beside my father. He stirs in his morphine sleep. And I dream for the first time in months. And in my dream we are walking, my father and I. He is leading me on a path I've never been on before. A path directly through a wash hidden from the roads and the subdivisions. The desert is barren, empty of cactus and brush. It is a place I've never seen and yet it is so close to somewhere I've known. My father mounts a horse and I continue walking beside him. The horse is regal, white as snow, healthy and tall. A horse fit for a prince. Gradually, as we walk, the horse weakens. His legs buckle. He grows cancer spots. The horse becomes frail as a baby until my father has to dismount and carry the horse in his arms. My father nods me on. There is still so much farther to go, he says to me.

I jump out of my chair. He stirs. I throw up acid. I vomit nothing. I thought often that it was his curse of hope to name me Ahlam, "dream," but perhaps it was his despair at waking life.

INSTEAD OF GOING TO the Winter Ball, we met Dylan by the reservation. Laura was wearing a short skirt and a crop top. I'd never seen her in heels. "I'm going to kiss Dylan tonight."

"He's so old," I said.

Dylan was waiting for us in his truck with the lights turned off. "Get in quick," he said. "I can't be parked here." Laura opened the door, got in beside him, and winked.

We took a dirt road that led into the darkness of the reservation. There were no homes or streetlights. The moon was waxing, nearly full and orange like a jack-o'-lantern. Laura pulled out a joint that she had tucked into her bra and blew smoke rings into Dylan's mouth.

"I'm getting out," I said. "Give me a cigarette."

I left them in the car and squatted beneath a paloverde. I couldn't think right. I'd never known desire, envy. I didn't even find Dylan handsome.

I put my cigarette out on my arm. I held it for a second and then made another burn. I wanted him to know I could wound myself too. I made three in all. A star cluster.

They were blue that night. They did not hurt until morning, infected and full of puss. They have faded to the color of my skin with the years. Now one is so faint, it is barely there. But the first two remain, wilted circles in my skin.

When I returned to the car, Laura's lipstick was smudged. But I had a scar Laura didn't. "Wanna go to a party?" she said. She was smiling like an idiot.

"Not going to a party with children," Dylan said.

"Please," she cried.

They passed a bottle of something between them while I veered my head to the right and to the left and into the rearview mirror to make sure no cops were around. Then we were merging onto the highway. "This is stupid far," I said.

"Look, the Superstitions!" Laura said.

"Look at the fucking moon. It's red," I said.

"Red moon apocalypse," Dylan said. He lifted Laura's locket from her chest. The locket was gold with a spiral of small sapphire jewels. "What's this pretty thing?"

Laura quickly batted it down again. Somehow she believed the quarter-sized locket covered her scar. "It was my mom's."

"*Was* your mom's?" he said.

"Yeah, before she shot herself."

"What? You told me she died of cancer," I said.

"I didn't want you to think I was a freak," she said.

"What was her name?" Dylan asked.

"Grace," Laura said slowly as if remembering something.

"Epic scar you got on your chest."

"I know," she said. "I was struck by lightning."

At the party, there was no furniture, only a single couch. The carpet smelled of liquor. There was a palm tree in the yard which waved innocently in the pale night wind. We didn't know anyone. They were all seniors.

Laura pulled me into the bathroom as soon as we entered. "You like Dylan, don't you?"

"I told you, he's old," I said.

"Good, because I'm afraid I like him so much I'll die," she said.

Everyone was drinking shots. Laura was already drunk and laughing, falling into Dylan. One of the boys pulled out some crumpled foil. He inhaled some powder from it. He looked elated with a secret. The foil was passed around to Laura.

"Here we go," Dylan said.

I grabbed Laura's wrist to pull her away, and she stuck her tongue out at me. I turned to the boy, his blond hair streaked blue. "What's it feel like?"

He looked at me as if I'd blared a flashlight in his face. "Midnight," he said and rolled his eyes.

Everyone began doing Jell-O shots. I realized that Laura and I were the only girls left. I finally took a shot, the cherry flavor faint against the cheap vodka, and tried not to gag. Someone shouted that the house was dry and who was going to make a beer run?

Dylan raised his hand. "But someone else has to drive."

"Please, please come with," Laura said to me.

I could follow the course of the night, or I could sit outside alone and wait for it all to unravel. I followed the plan. One night was longer than a week in those days. One night wasn't like all the other nights, the way it was later when I'd known the night too well and too hard.

In the car, the boy with the blond hair streaked blue ranted on about Jesus and crystal and the desert. In her hummingbird voice, Laura sang the song on the radio, "Blue American." She rolled down the window to smoke a cigarette. "No one is dying," she said to me. "You can stop being so serious." Dylan kept turning from the passenger seat to stroke Laura's thigh. I cringed when his forefinger shot up beneath her skirt.

The boy was swerving, driving his parents' Mercedes over curbs and nearly into a stop sign. I could hear my mother's voice in my head. I could hear her disappointment, which was worse than her anger. I wished we had gone to the Winter Ball, that I was dancing with some boy whose voice still squeaked, who had no burn wounds, no car, no stories about birds dying in the wild of the woods.

Back at the house at last, I went into the kitchen and poured the rest of the Bacardi that was there, 151 proof. It burned going down. I liked the feeling. I liked it like I liked the burns I had made on my arm. I felt carved out. I covered my eyes. Four shots in and I was blind.

———

IT BEGAN WITH THAT first vision of Laura. The voices uttering inarticulately in my head. The violent hiss would rise and send my entire skull into an underwater uproar. It was a nightmare orchestra of the mind. I heard them again beneath the palm tree outside of the party that night of the Winter Ball. They were voices longing for a body, the voices of the dead.

When I learned to drive, the voices would erupt suddenly. I

had to bear the screaming through my urge to run my car off
the road. The voices commanded me: *Join us. Make it quiet.* It
happened always at the same bend, the one I can see just ahead
from the hospital room window, where the highway curves
away from the reservation and the last view of my mountain
is subsumed by the road walls. The desert, its darkness, was
as inviting as the ocean. If you could just dive into it, you
could also disappear. I tried to dance these voices off, lose my
mind inside of the fierceness of a turn. Only alcohol faded the
voices, as if a fan was turned on.

But I've survived. I know only to survive.

THEY TOOK US INTO separate rooms. Dylan and Laura on
one side of the house. The blond, blue-streaked boy and
I on another. I blacked out. When I came to, shortly past
dawn, the stranger was staring at the drawn blinds that
led to the porch, his face clenched. He was not crying. Not
speaking of Jesus and crystal and the brilliant endurance of
the saguaro without rain and the coldness of February. He
was still, as if asleep with his eyes open.

My grey panties were ripped and lying beside me. There
was a pain between my legs that resembled hunger more
than soreness. We lay on nothing but a sheet. His jeans were
crumpled at his ankles, and his wife-beater was stained with
sweat. I grabbed my underwear and stuffed them into my bag.

"What's your name?" he said when I got to the door.

"Ariel," I said.

I ran across the house. One door was cracked open. Laura was alone, awake. She pushed down the covers and rolled over naked to reveal the sheets below. I saw the scar on her chest for the first time in the light. It was scarlet. I saw the blondish-reddish hair tangled at her groin, contrasted against her caramel skin. So little of her seemed of her father.

"Is there a lot of blood?" she asked.

"Only a few drops."

"He left this," she said and crumpled a piece of paper into her bag. "And some money."

In the afternoon, it is said that a woman's face with long, flowing hair emerges on the rocks of the mountain my father named for me. Others say that it is the face of Jesus. It is a desert upon which each of us projected a different delusion. Laura told me that the tribe her mother descended from would not utter the names of their children from age ten until marriage, and would never utter the names of the dead, and that this was why Indian graves were unmarked. She told me she learned of this too late, while wandering into the reservation and meeting three young boys who told her in the middle of hide-and-go-seek she'd come to a terrible death if she told them her name. And so, she told me, it was that day she went by Laura and not her birth name, and she would go by it until betrothed.

But Laura was never married. Laura was never Laura.

The morning I found those grey cotton panties beside me, I began to go by another name, a name once used for cover on the Superstitions where my father and I found ourselves lost years before. I thought this might mean I would never be hunted again.

Laura and I took anything we could find in that house. We counted thirty-seven bucks, a CD collection, a pager. We called a cab. I wanted her to get in ahead of me. To wave me in. There was only one taxi service I knew, my father's. For a moment, through the window of that house, I thought I saw him in the driver's seat, though I knew his shift was long over.

I walked out onto the porch and saw everything from the night before. An empty pack of cigarettes on a lawn chair, bottles on the counter. I hid behind the palm tree.

"Come on," Laura said. "It's okay." As we drove away, I watched the Superstitions disappear in the rearview mirror.

"Laura, look," I said. "There's snow on the mountains."

"Don't look back," she said. "It's bad luck."

I wished I could reverse time, erase the night. I wished for a fata morgana to reveal itself floating above the desert, another land to which we could go.

Laura interrupted my thoughts. "Can't believe it. No goodbye, nothing."

"What's on the piece of paper?" I said.

"An address in New York," she muttered.

"What an asshole." I touched her arm. "Leaving money like you're some whore."

"It was for the cab, stupid," she snapped.

"I didn't have a great time, either. Thanks for asking," I said. We remained quiet until the cab pulled off the highway.

"I'm sorry. Sometimes it feels like some crazy beast lives in me," she said. I rolled down the window and wished the cold air on my face was water, washing the night off me.

"What do you remember about New York?" she asked. I stuck my head out and let the wind take my hair and drown out her voice.

"Please tell me something, anything," she said. "I'm dying."

"There it's really February," I said at last, and then, thinking of my snow globe, my only false memory of New York, added, "and right now there is a woman, and she is walking between the tall buildings through a snowstorm. And it is quiet because the snow quiets everything. Someday she will be me. Someday I'll get the fuck out of here."

"Let me come with you," she said.

The cab dropped us off at the entrance to the reservation. We walked into it. I puked red in the lifting lavender. Laura held my hair back. "I want to die," I said.

"Did you finally earn your blow job girl title?" she asked and put her fingers to the creases of my lips, cleaning away the vomit. I pulled my sleeve up my arm to reveal the burns I had done. "Did he do this to you?"

I shook my head. The pain suddenly announced itself everywhere. Laura kissed my skin just beside the wounds. "What day is it even?"

I knew it was Sunday.

"You ever heard of that song 'Gloomy Sunday'?" Laura said. "It was this really beautiful song. So beautiful it caused, like, a hundred people to commit suicide in the thirties."

Laura began to hum as she had the night I met her. As she did every day I knew her.

"Be quiet. Did you hear that?" I said. "Sounds like a firework just went off."

"Or a gun," she said gazing toward the mountains in the east. "Look, it's another day."

APRIL

THE SAGUAROS WERE EVERYWHERE scattered like crucifixes against the sky, endless and ancient, and in the half-light cast human shadows on the dust. Their arms were cast forth, cheerfully upright, blossoming come April, until dying or struck by lightning and stripped to skeletons. When we left on drives in the mountains and gained elevation, the saguaro would disappear, and when we returned, my father would scream, "I saw it first!" of the first saguaro seen, and we would know we were near home.

That Sunday, after the Winter Ball I never attended, my father found me in the living room tearing a piece of bread apart and told me to get in the car. We were going to see some snow. In the woods two hours north, it had already melted, but the weather was so completely different, crisp and mountainous, it was enough to feel I had left the night behind.

As we descended into the valley, the radio signal returned.

Drifting in and out of a dreamless sleep, I heard the news of the final suicide. He must have driven after Laura and me, because at dawn, the boy with blue-streaked hair pulled into his parents' garage, parked his car at their mansion that bordered the reservation, took off his jeans, his stained shirt, unlocked the safe that held his father's old service pistol, walked out into the desert, put the gun into his mouth, and pulled the trigger.

Laura did not call. She waited at Starbucks, knowing I would come. The American madness of it all, our sitting at the local Starbucks counting deaths. I sat down next to her and plugged my fingers through the wire tabletop. She rolled a cigarette toward me.

"I think it's time to disappear to Mexico," she whispered. "Or we're next."

"It's like a curse," I said.

Laura's mascara had leaked beneath her eyes. She'd been crying. I couldn't tell if it was her hands or my hands shaking the table or if the entire world was shaking, a sudden earthquake. "This happens in lots of places you know. People getting shot, people dying. It's normal."

"You just said it yourself: 'or we're next.'"

"Maria will help us. We'll go to her. She'll tell us what to do," Laura said.

We spent the months before Mexico smoking dramatically over chai lattes. I had cut off all my hair as girls do, believing it might destroy the past. Trevor's mother still came every few days, speaking in a hushed voice to her psychics. Laura sat at the corner table with her violin, waiting for me to finish dance class. Sometimes when we stayed after closing, she would play and I would dance on pointe in the handicap parking spot.

It was in the Starbucks bathroom that we took our first pregnancy tests. "Would your baby be, like, half dead?" Laura said as we waited over the pee sticks. She shook her minus sign several times even after the allotted two minutes had passed, half hoping, perhaps, for a different result.

"And what would yours be?" I said. "Half alien?"

Spring break came, and we drove to Mexico, Laura and I both in the backseat, her father driving. He played the Mexican stations and hummed beneath his breath. When we followed his trail those days in the desert, I never saw his face and figured it stern. But his eyes were watery and green and lopsided, and there was a sadness locked thick and old in them. No matter the season, his face was always burned. He drove as if he were all alone in the car, fast, pushing the speedometer to ninety miles per hour, paying no notice even when Laura rolled down the window to smoke a cigarette, the wind lashing our skin.

Near the border, Laura used the bathroom at a gas station. Her father turned to me and said, "Laura, she takes after her mother."

We left Laura's father at the hotel bar and walked down the beach. There were mansions being built, a luxury spa named

Castle Sonora. A ship had wrecked and was left on the sand. The sun poured through its rusted hull. Locals passed us selling jewelry, ashtrays, clay pots, and holding signs of sunburned blondes with braids. Donkeys trailed after them. White teenagers zigzagged over the beach in their ATVs like mosquitoes. The engines drowned out the ocean's smell and sound.

"If all else fails, we could always live on that ship," Laura said.

"How would we make money?" I asked.

"Oh, that's easy. We'd be blow job girls."

By nightfall, we reached the end of the peninsula and the only bar on the beach. It was full of people we knew. The same popular kids were sitting at a central table on the patio as they did at our high school three hours north. Laura ordered margaritas, and we took them and sat on a ledge that faced the sea. Locals on the beach played accordions and trumpets, muffled by the speakers' top one hundred hits. I was sun-kissed, feeling drowsy, almost pretty with a tan, romantic.

"Should we try to talk to anyone?" I asked.

"These humans?" Laura gulped the rest of her drink. As she bounced off the ledge, a senior tumbled into her and vomited onto the arm of a child selling sticks of gum.

"Fuckface, are you blind?" Laura screamed.

"What, spic? You talking to me?" He wiped his mouth.

"Here, chica." He handed the child a nickel. "Gimme a gum."

"You know the most common phrase in the movies is 'let's get out of here'?" Laura had already slipped off her skirt and begun to run toward the sea. She screamed for me to follow.

"What about the tide?" I had never been in the ocean. It was such a sweet tug, the pull of the sand beneath my toes. The sea purred. The music from the bar was reduced to a faint hymn beneath the wind. There were sailboats a short distance from us, docked for the night. I could see the trace of a man's arm, the ember of his cigarette as he drew it to his mouth and ashed over the side of the boat.

"Get in!" Laura splashed me. The salt stung my eyes. I slipped out of my jean shorts and dove into the water after her. Laura lay on her back and floated on the waves. I kicked my legs frantically beside her, desperate for the sea floor to remain in reach.

"Just lie down. It's like bathwater. Pretend you're dead," she said.

"I'd rather not."

"But you're missing the stars," she said.

I lay back into the waves and choked as the water poured into my mouth. "Going back to the beach."

I knew even then that the moment illustrated the essential difference between us—Laura could lie back and regard the stars as the ocean swarmed beneath her, and I could not, my feet unsecured from the sand.

"Dylan would have stayed," she said as the calm waves urged me to shore.

Maria lived in a small house on the side of town beyond the railway tracks where all the wild dogs roamed. Maria spoke only in Spanish and to Laura. She looked at me and murmured. Her face was impossibly white against her suntanned body. Her long ash-grey hair resolved at the hips of her dress. She held her palms open in her lap. On one was drawn the *hamsa*, the Arabic amulet against the evil eye. She pointed at it and looked at me and spoke.

Laura turned to me. "Maria saw you coming. She says not to be afraid. What happens . . . happens. Maria says we are sisters. She says you may be afraid of me, but that I am here to protect and guide you in this life. And to teach you a lesson . . ." Laura drifted. Then Maria turned to Laura and spoke only to her, handing her a small purse. I understood only one word in the stream, *Sonora*.

Maria took out a large piece of paper and some charcoal. She began to draw. With her hands, she motioned for us to leave her. I walked outside into the bright heat, waiting for Laura to follow me back onto the dirt road. "Not yet," Laura said. "This is for you. Maria said they will protect you. And that we have to wait here."

The purse was full of stones. We sat down on a large

boulder and kicked gravel at each other. The stones began to stain my hands black. A starving dog approached, searching a pile of trash for food, whimpering at us.

An hour must have passed. Maria was so quiet that I didn't hear her approach. She touched my shoulder and handed me the drawing.

On it were two figures, two girls, hand in hand. They were both dressed in long-sleeved funereal gowns, everything about them the same, but the one on the left had a face like my own and the one on the right had the face of a skeleton. The rest of the drawing was filled with black birds and bottles, indiscriminate figures dancing, a swarm of arbitrary life.

"I see soul," Maria said in accented English. "Some of your soul in underworld, other soul here."

That night we lay in the humid hotel bed, and I listened to Laura's breath rise against the ocean. I did not sleep. The image Maria drew stayed with me like a nightmare. I was afraid to fall unconscious for fear of what I might see.

Toward dawn, I shook Laura. "You told her to draw that stuff," I said.

Laura's eyes half opened, but she was still asleep. "Are you there?" she murmured.

Our last night at the bar, Laura left me to swim once again. I ordered a Coke and played with the stones, watching my red flesh turn inky. I felt someone approach and then his elbow brush mine. "Hey," he said. "I like your hair short like that."

"Thanks," I said. He handed me his drink. The ice melted, the salt stung my lips. He was twice my height, healthy and broad shouldered and tan, wearing sandals and a backward cap. His hair was brown but lightened by the sun. He smiled with his eyes. He had a small mole on his cheek. He was the antithesis of Dylan, of the blue-streaked blond.

"I've seen you around school," he said. I nodded. "Aren't you, like, a ballerina?"

"Sort of," I said.

"I'm Eli."

"I know," I said. I thought he had come to save my life.

"Who's Señor Guapo?" Laura said, returning from the beach.

On the drive home, to the soundtrack of Mexican ballads, I daydreamed of Eli arched over me by moonlight. The sea at our toes. I was wind in the fantasy. I was not in the car. I choreographed an entire dance in the backseat full of swirls and leaps and knee falls. At the end of it all, I'd just lie down on the stage. I'd float.

"What are you dreaming about?" Laura said at last. The first saguaros had long since appeared.

"Oh, just dance," I said.

"For a second you looked in love, but maybe that's just because I am . . . helplessly."

That was the year I turned seventeen, that I got my driver's license, the year the millennium changed over, the world didn't end, and my parents bought a house.

Every afternoon I sat beside the fountain in the garden. We could not afford a pool. I compulsively checked the tan lines between my lower abdomen and my belly. It was the first time in my life I felt pretty. Only the flight of movements could approximate my adoration for Eli, a grand jeté en tournant throughout the dry washes that ran through our new neighborhood, the fouetté by sunset, the fouetté so much like love in its dazzled spinning.

My obsession was fantastic. It smothered the year's darkness. I hid Maria's drawing in a closet with my old children's books, praying for the day that so much time had passed I'd forget where I had stowed it.

I CANNOT SLEEP SO I walk to the window of my father's hospital room. In the distance, I spot Eli's old neighborhood. Somewhere, in a car, a young couple is driving toward their first night of love. I no longer know anyone in Arizona. There is no one I can call. In this hospital room, my father's heart is the soundtrack of my unsleep.

I try to imagine Laura here at the window, smoking a

cigarette, the way she would between her middle and ring fingers rather than the way everyone else does between index and middle. She says something to me like, "Stop being so dark," though she is the one who looks so sad. I think of the ocean. Of the desert as ocean. And this works to calm me. At least the ocean covers up all its death.

———

MY FATHER TURNED SIXTY. We had a dinner at my house that included my mom, our newest kitten Sharmut, and my father's only friend, the waiter Tomás from the restaurant Galileo, with whom he returned from the porch in a cloud of marijuana smoke. "I was showing Tomás the beautiful fountain," my father said. "Oh, put this song up, Rachel. This is my favorite song. Dance with me, Ahlami . . . This is really a song about a love that will never be."

"Dad," I said.

"What, you don't think once your father was very charming? This is The Cure. They like to wear all black like you."

"Stop!"

"Don't embarrass her," my mother said.

"Remembering you standing silence in the rain, as I came to your heart and felt love," he sang.

"Those aren't even the right lyrics," I said.

"You are right. That is because I don't understand English. I am an alien. I was born walking, born in the nowhere between galaxies. The Middle East is like a big black hole," he said, his eyes red, stoned. "Maybe they should have left me in the road on the way to Damascus. Maybe I would have been mistaken as a Jewish baby. That would have been better. Much better. Then you would have been a rich little girl, and I would know all the right words to the songs."

"Here he goes again," my mother said.

"Black holes—I have a theory about that," Tomás said.

"Can I speak to my daughter?" my father said.

"You obviously can't," my mother said.

My father turned to me. "You look too skinny again. You got sick in Mexico?"

"I'm fine," I said.

"Sometimes I worry," he said, shaking his head. "Sometimes I worry curses just go on forever. Do you know what a black hole is, Ahlami?"

"I'm sure Tomás can tell us all about it," I said.

"They are places in the center of all universes, the places where all the light comes in and never escapes," Tomás said. "But I have my doubts. There is no place where there is no light."

"Just give me a hug for my birthday," my father said. "I'll squeeze some of my fat into you."

I thought of Eli impatiently as I leaned into my father's shoulder. I knew it was a moment that I should concentrate on, memorize, a moment I would one day miss. It was the first time I noticed my father's smell had changed. Its briskness, the spearmint of his cologne had less power. It was moldier, muskier.

LIKE FACES, THE SMELL of a person cannot be replicated. The smell of a fire in my hair from a particular party, the smell of a friend's perfume rubbed into my shirt. The smell of lipstick and chalk soaking the dressing rooms at dance rehearsals. The smell of a lover in your fingernails the morning after. The smell of my mother: orange peel, suntan lotion, faint vanilla. The smell of Laura: lavender laundry detergent, danger, linger of red wine, sweat, cigarette. The smell of Eli: the smell of seventeen, of the beach at night, coconut, white blossom, salt, stars. The smell of Dylan: vodka, fire, dirt in autumn, February in the desert.

The smell of my father: Ralph Lauren Safari, cumin, tobacco, spearmint, musk, red meat. Home.

My father awakens for a moment. He is nauseous, in pain. He calls me by my mother's name. I run down the hall for the night nurse. As I run, I remember my dream, of a mariachi band placing me in a coffin to sail on a dark expanse of water. Laura was with them, dressed in their costume. The songs they sang were intoxicating, the kind of songs you cannot help but dance to, the kind of songs that make you feel drunk, your head heavy and swinging. A song that makes you yearn to fall through the floor or soar on a carpet. A song that makes you want to smash glass.

The nurse pours some water, gives my father a pill. "He needs another painkiller," she says. My face changes. "It's normal, hon."

I try to remember the song, the singing still in my bones, but I cannot remember the words. My loves have always been seared with this singing, this singing written by death, the way some lands have always been crippled by war.

—————

AFTER MEXICO, I SAW Eli alone only twice. The first time he picked me up from school, I told Laura that I was helping him with his math homework. "That's cool. I'm going to go home and respond to Dylan's letter," she said. I knew there was no letter.

In Eli's roofless jeep, we drove up into the seat of the McDowell Mountains and parked yards away from the playground where Laura, Dylan, and I lay and smoked and spoke of the disappeared boys in the Estrella Mountains. I followed Eli on a trail that wound steeply uphill until we were halfway up the mountain. His hand stretched behind his body, expectant for mine. We stopped and looked out at the valley, streaks of sun piercing the hump of Camelback Mountain. He swiped my cheek affectionately. "There's a smile," he said.

Farther up, there was a sign: DO NOT GO OFF THE TRAIL. SENSITIVE HABITAT. Eli leaped off the path into the crevasse.

"It says don't do that," I said.

"This scares you, and cigarettes don't?" He laughed.

I peered into the ditch. At the end of it was a small cave. Eli kept going on into it, ducking from the brush, his skin perfectly tanned, turning for me with a teasing smile, his gait long and elegant as a horse in ceremony, hardly making a sound in the rocks.

I watched him and thought with this man I will have three babies. With this man I will have a beautiful home. A beautiful car. With this man I will never want. With this man I will never be sad again.

I sat on a rock in the shade. My hands began to tingle, my cheeks. I wanted to batter my head into the mountain wall. Water began to rush around my feet. It roared forth. The boulder above the crevasse was quaking. A mountain lion thrashed up the mountain in the distance. Eli was nowhere. Hundreds of rattlesnakes had slipped out from their homes in the dust.

I was still on the rock when Eli kissed my forehead, the smell of his skin and his shirt stirring me. "I found an arrowhead for you."

The arrowhead was just a stone with a sharp point at one end, not chiseled. There was nothing special about it. It did not matter. He had taken his shirt off, and I was filled with desire for him. I yearned to run my hands over him like cool marble, his body so chiseled but for a single scar on his lower abdomen. "That looks like a barbwire fence."

"My appendix," he said.

With Eli, I betrayed Laura. I fled our pact with sadness, our pact with blood. My parents too had a pact with sadness. I knew, even so young, that bliss couldn't last. After my parents bought the house, they fought even more. We finally owned land. We belonged. The Second Intifada was on the television. Ariel Sharon's face was constantly in our living room, in sunglasses at the Temple Mount surrounded by soldiers. When they fought, I went into my room. I practiced my steps. One—two-three. Two—two-three. Three—. Échappé, chasse, grand jeté. Eli's hands, Eli's lips, Eli's voice. Repetition as a means to block out the wreckage.

My father resumed painting on his new porch. He liked the sound of the fountain. He said it was almost like being at the sea. It helped him think. He made a painting called *Indian in the Woods*. The painting was a swirl of beige and blue, the colors of the sea and the desert. He said his Indian was trapped. He didn't recognize anything in the forest, the Indian; he didn't recognize himself.

"All you can see wherever you go is where you came from. This is the torture of exile," my father said. The paint stained the porch of our new garden. My mother scrubbed for days but couldn't get it out. One afternoon, she stood in front of the television for an hour without saying anything. This was her only protest. My father walked to the living room and crashed the bureau of china onto the floor. "You and your fucking people, Rachel. You are never satisfied," he screamed. "When will my suffering end?"

My mother lunged, trying to save her inheritance. Her feet already bled from the shards. She sat there all night among the broken plates murmuring, *Why me, why me*. From forty, there were three that remained intact.

I called Eli. I asked him to come save my life.

Eli lived on a road called Via del Paraiso. The drive to his house is still my favorite, along Pima Road that runs along the reservation where once it was without casino or training stadium—empty and dark. Back then, there were no street-lights on that stretch. After Eli, I drove the road with my sunroof down and all my windows open in a certain ecstasy, imagining the dark expanse at my side was ocean, tempting fate by looking up instead of ahead, counting the stars.

The perfume of candles wafted out of his house. Gardenia, jasmine. Always the scent of white blossoms and the sea. The sea still in your hair by night. Eli walked me to his room, so close I was trembling, as if the moon were something we held between our hips. It was full and splashed onto his bed. Eli said nothing before he took off my shirt, skirt, and slipped off my shoes. He kissed the inside of my arm, the burns smaller, paled. I heard the sea. He didn't notice my scars. The gold cross he wore around his neck tickled my breast as we made love.

When we were finished, I traced the circles of sweat along his back. The here-and-there mole. The back is such a canvas of wonders when you are in love. I could not sleep for fear he'd stop breathing. I watched his rib cage fall into the sheets and rise up as the night gave way to the dawn. I first understood why Christians prayed for a savior in the form of a beautiful man. He had absolved me of the blue-streaked blond.

It was all so foolish then, as it is now, as it is forever. To be in love with beauty. To try to hold on to it.

Soon after we finished, I said, "I feel so at home."

He never answered me. He was already asleep.

Eli did not call the next day. Eli was not at school the day after that. I yearned to tell Laura what had happened, to scream it to the entire school, but Laura did not appear at the bleachers after third period, at the library, or at our window at lunch. I waited for Eli in the lot where he usually parked his jeep. I sat there until nightfall when a janitor told me it was time to go. On Tuesday, there was a crackle from the intercom right after we recited the Pledge of Allegiance. We could hear the principal coughing, the muffled sound of a suppressed sob. Everyone shuffled their papers. The teacher excused herself to the bathroom. Moments later, we heard the principal's voice again, restrained, but clear. "Yesterday morning, students . . ." he began.

An early morning April storm caused a flash flood that cascaded down from the mountains, filling the washes with rain. Eli lost his footing. He was caught, bones shattered, in the arms of a saguaro cactus thirty feet below. He was in a coma.

I left school immediately. At the hospital, I saw his mother at his side, lying over his sleeping legs. I watched through the blinds, knowing I'd never say anything.

The saguaro cactus accumulates its weight because it stores water. Much of the water the desert gets is housed inside that crucifix of a dead tree. Perhaps the needles that held Eli in his last sleep released rainwater. From above and below, he was covered in rain.

———

I CANNOT SLEEP. I kiss my father's cheek. I leave the hospital to smoke. The receptionist eyes me. I say hello. She tells me I should cut back. I nod. I use my phone as a flashlight once on the reservation. I draw a light show across the paloverde. I try to draw the faces of those I have lost. All I see are tree veins, the insides of us all.

A raccoon appears. He sneaks between the trees. His eyes are red in the dark, his face thick as a carnival mask. I remain still. I throw my cigarette at him. "Don't make me see," I scream. I hear Laura's voice explaining to me the shamanic power of the raccoon: shape-shifters, owners of secrets, messengers from the land of the dead.

The reservation stretches on before me. I see no people. I see only the casino, the reflection of headlights from the highway scanning the desert like a warning. I long for people. I long to run into the desert and find a fire around which people are sitting. The Deir Yassin massacre took place a few days before my father's birth. It was anomalous in its violence. Villagers, women, children, all were shot. Town after town from Jerusalem to the northern borders emptied as people left on foot with only their most important belongings, thinking they'd be back soon. Some were lucky enough to board buses, the way only a few years earlier, my mother's grandparents boarded trains in the green woods across Eastern Europe toward a far worse fate. I look out at the reservation, still and glittering with casinos, and think of all the death dried up and buried in its dirt. Nightmares always recur but never our most beautiful dreams.

I am a memory house for those I have lost, those I no longer know. I try to stop it, try to stop the vision of Eli through the blinds, but it persists like a compulsion. The yellowed skin, the latex sweat, the heart monitor beeps ensuring that Eli's life beat on inside his sleeping body through the blinded window. I remember prom weeks after he died—mascara-stained face, grey dress, weeping in the bathroom, Laura in the stall, pouring me tequila and vodka and schnapps all mixed up in one water bottle, and I still taste the liquor, and I remember wanting to flee her, and being unable to flee her, so in need of her and half hating her for it, and I still am nauseous from it. I hear that beep still through the hospital blinds. I hear it resound from every room I pass. I hear it and fear every room in the hospital contains someone

I love. Someone I've lost or will lose. This is my heaven. This is my hell. God keeping our hearts in check. Forever and ever, amen.

I am no longer able to shut my eyes, no longer able to hide. I cannot flee the hospital room. I go into the last moments of the ones I love. The Rolodex of faces shuffles to the end and begins again. I pass their rooms. I want to be inside, not on the outside looking in. These are the cracks where all the ghosts live. And the cracks are everywhere. I go there with them, to their ends, again and again. I go in case they are listening, so they know they are not alone.

<hr />

AFTER I LEFT ELI at the hospital, I walked for miles into the reservation. The heat had risen past one hundred degrees. I had no water. I had no phone. I wept like a lunatic. I spoke to myself. There was no escape. I was cursed. I wanted the voices. I wanted a sign. I wanted to see something.

I walked and walked and did not see a single person. I didn't see any sign of life. No sign demanding I stay on one path and not another. The desert was silent as a graveyard. I was not thirsty. I was not tired. I came home after dark, my leg covered in jumping cholla needles, my feet raw with blisters. My father was sitting on the hood of his taxi, smoking. My mother was at the window. I saw her face was swollen from crying. "Don't ever disappear like that," my father said in a half yell. I knew he was getting old. He had spent his quota of anger on the broken china. "This pain, it will pass," he said. "Trust me. It will pass."

Laura was on our couch. She had a yellow rose. "Well." She paused. "Now we are together again." Now we are together again.

Laura and I snuck out for the first time since Dylan and walked to the cemetery. "I spoke to him only once," she said.

"I think I loved him," I said.

"I said, 'Señor Guapo, don't break my sister's heart.'"

We jumped the tawny wall that was the boundary between an apartment complex and the cemetery. The grass was well mowed and sprayed with chemicals so that it did not resemble a desert cemetery but a cemetery in New England or upstate New York, a cemetery that might look natural in another locale. There was a large pond that reflected the moon. We lay down as the sprinklers came on. Laura hummed and drew her nails down my arm as I cried.

I heard the *whoosh* of a car that sounded like tires on wet asphalt. I looked up and saw a white Lincoln swerve off the cemetery road and head toward us. I screamed for Laura to get up.

The headlights blinded me. Laura did not move. I stumbled and scratched my legs and elbows on the tawny wall of the complex. "It's a cop!" I screamed.

But when I turned my head again, perched on the wall,

about to leap into the parking lot, the car was gone. "Didn't you see that car?"

"We've got to get you out of here," she said. "It's not just this. I've been seeing my mom lately in my dreams, but the weird thing is . . . in the dreams, she really, really looks like you."

AUGUST

IT WAS LONG PAST midnight. It hadn't yet rained, but we could smell the sage and the smoke of creosote in the air. We could smell the honeysuckle and the dust. Laura and I drove off a side road into the mountains. We were leaving for New York in the morning.

That last summer we were pizza delivery girls, and we'd drive to mansions and get tipped big by the husbands and eyed sideways by the wives. We swept the floors. We flattened the dough. We smoked pot with our manager in the parking lot. He spoke about Hamlet and how the East Coast was full of pretentious assholes—that this was why he dropped out of Brown. In the evenings, I would dance at a studio that had gone out of business a block from my house. No one bothered to lock up. Laura would come and play as I spun.

That last night, I sat on the roof of my car chain-smoking and drawing original constellations from the sudden spread of stars. Laura pulled out a CD from her bag and put it into the deck. "Tell me if you like this," she said. It was instrumental, at first all violin, laced with her voice humming a dark fairy tale. She got out of the car and stripped to her unmatched bra and underwear. "It's too hot."

The music was of winter, true winter, the quiet blanket of the sky shedding itself in white. And her cooing, thick with spells.

"You're going to be famous," I said. "You're going to be my famous friend."

"Will you be my groupie forever?" She was walking toward the hills on tiptoe as if not to wake the sleeping desert.

———✦✦✦———

MY MOTHER RETURNS TO the hospital at four in the morning, shakes me awake. For a moment I am in high school again. I'm late for work, late for school. I've never woken well. My mother would pour ice water over me, strip the blankets off the bed, set four alarms.

"Let's take a drive," she says.

"Now?" I ask.

"I can't sleep."

We drive through the dark. We drive as we always did when I was a kid, me in the passenger seat. There is no traffic, not even police. The lights take five minutes to turn. The mountains hover in the distance, sleeping giants forgotten in the sweep of streets and homes.

"Do you need a bra? Or your hair cut?" she says. "We can get our nails done."

I turn some music on. I watch her face from the corner of my eyes. I see the way in which her skin has closed in around her jaws. The crow's-feet sharpened, her hair nearly all grey. She is trying not to cry. I see that it is true, that I've grown up to look like her. I recall the hundreds of drives in the passenger seat with her, an older version of the same Japanese make of this car, the same grey color. Me turning the music on, her trying to speak. Her asking me if I'd done my homework, why did I dress in such dark clothes, why was I so dark, why I couldn't make a friend outside of Laura.

"When will anything just be okay?" she asks.

"No one is going to save us," I say. I turn the music up and light a cigarette.

"You should quit smoking," she says. "You look worn for how young you are."

"Thanks, Mom," I say.

She begins to cough. I hold my cigarette out the window but do not throw it out. For years, I've tried to catch the hourly differences, the day-to-day aging. But the only discernible difference is that my mother began to appear in my reflection. I was becoming less myself and more her, and more my father on the inside. One morning, I saw my mother in my silhouette. My face had narrowed, grown thinner.

There is lightning in the distance. The sky is purple for a moment. I am lost in thought with nothing so beautiful. That I am not close to thirty, and that I have a face people might describe as charactered.

"It's going to storm, Mom," I say.

"Can I get a cigarette?"

IT WAS LONG PAST midnight. Laura's music played on. It was composed in the language of stars, tinkling in a crystal pool suspended from the constellations. She used chimes now and then, the chimes that characterized every patio in Arizona, the piano, trees combed by wind. A prelude to a storm. It was like discovering the secret room in a dream of your house that holds all the magic. It was music I wished I lived inside. Around us, cactus, hills filled with jumping cholla, the heat of August like another animal heaving over us.

Laura was nearly naked in the dark, and the moon cast a sliver of light across her thin chest. She disappeared into the hills. When I looked up, she had hiked atop one of the hills that emanated from the higher peaks and spread out her arms. Her hair fell back with her head. The breeze purred through the brush and up through the mountains. "You should come down!" I yelled.

In Laura's purse, I found a large envelope. In it was a stack of photographs bounded with one of her scrunchies. I flicked her hair from my hands. She took the photographs the day we decided we were going to New York. It was the day my ballet teacher Françoise called to tell me the bad news about a video I had sent to a company in Los Angeles. Françoise had said, "We must be honest. Your legs are a few inches too short. Your turnout is not perfect. I think you must begin to think about modern companies."

Laura was lying beside me in the hall of our school beside the window, the long legs she inherited from her father sprawled ungracefully. Her body, effortlessly thin. I grew up wishing I could change my bones into hers, wishing I could change the only thing of myself that would last.

"What's wrong?" she asked.

"Didn't get the audition."

"Let's just leave," she said as if it were the simplest thing in the world. As if that was the solution to an imperfect turnout. "We're almost eighteen. We can go to New York. In New York they will love you. They will love us."

In the photos, Laura and I were dancing in the desert. The mountains were in the distance. The day was grey. We were caught mid-movement, our edges blurred. In the images, the skin was not my own. Laura superimposed her lightning scar all over my body and spread it throughout her own. In the images, we shared identical surfaces, identical alien skin.

She titled each image after a constellation. My favorite was Cygnus in which our surfaces were blue.

On the mountain, where we stayed long past midnight on our last evening in Arizona, there was lightning in the distance. "It's going to storm, Laura," I shouted.

"Just one last cigarette here," she said.

Watching her there, her arms spread, I recalled the way I saw Laura as a child on the Superstition Mountains, crucified upside down from a cactus. Watching her, her body posed like a scarecrow, I remembered something else—a sudden fact from a history class, that it was in those same mountains, a hundred years earlier, that a colonel staged a siege on the Yavapai community. Trying to escape the rain of gunfire and shrapnel, hundreds rushed into a cave to hide. The colonel and his soldiers pushed boulders in front of the entrance, killing by starvation whomever their bullets did not reach. When the boulders were at last removed from the cave, decades later, all that remained were the skeletons of the hundreds who had perished. I remembered too that this was where we had come with Dylan, but the playground was gone.

MY MOTHER TURNS THE music down. "I want to speak to you. We never talk anymore."

"We've been talking all day," I say.

"Tell me something about your life, anything."

"You know all there is to know."

"Fine." For a moment she is quiet. "Fine. I'll talk about me. Soon I'll be fifty. I have not been on a trip in twenty years. Your father is in the hospital. I only have you. No brothers, no sisters. No parents. I can't keep the pounds off anymore. I keep thinking where did I go wrong, why did I choose this life? Why did I choose your father? Why me? And I know what's going to happen to me: in a few years I'll get Alzheimer's or something worse, and I won't care that the weight won't come off, and I won't feel sad, and maybe I won't remember how much it hurts that you and your father prefer your silent spells while all these years I've had no one to talk to."

"Mom!" I shout.

"After all that we gave you, how could you let Laura destroy your life?"

LAURA FINALLY DESCENDED THE mountain. We sat on the hood of the car. A coyote appeared in the distance, sniffing the dust. Laura howled. The coyote vanished into the hills.

"The playground's gone," I said.

She bent down and scooped up a pile of sand, let it fall from her hands. The rain had begun. She swayed in the wind. "Get up. Last rain dance," she said. "One last bloodbath."

We cursed the desert. We cursed the years. We cursed the high school. We lured the storm to come on stronger. We demanded more. We were howling with want, jumping cholla sprawled about us.

For a minute, the sky was purple, the dust rose. Laura kept screaming, whipping her head in the breeze of branches. I wished at that moment I could stop it. I wished I could make us quiet. Stop our want.

"Fuck," Laura screamed.

Water rushed down the mountain. We leaped into the car. The rain was thick. We could not see the road through the dust. We switched the headlights on and off. The car skidded from the force of the water. A branch from a saguaro was struck by lightning right ahead of us. The rain finally extinguished the fire. I clutched Laura's hand.

"This is it," Laura said. We watched the violent dance of the trees, enraptured. It only ever lasted a few moments, the rain. Its brevity was its magic.

"Dylan thinks we're just staying a few days," Laura said and lit a cigarette, puffing pretty circles, testing me.

"How are we going to pay for somewhere to stay?" I said. The last lightning turned everything purple, then returned us to the night.

"I have three hundred dollars saved," she said, looking into the storm. "You see that in the distance? Looks like it's a piece of curtain waving about. That's La Llorona."

"Three hundred dollars is nothing, Laura."

"Maybe, but maybe not," she said. "So the story goes Llorona's husband left her for another woman, so she drowned her children for revenge and then killed herself. But the gods wouldn't let her into heaven unless she could show them her kids. So she stalks the desert looking for other children to bring to the afterlife. Beware of the mistress, Maria always said, weeping, in the howl of the August monsoons."

MY MOTHER PULLS THE car to the side of the road just beside the canal. "Why don't you drive? I'm too upset."

I take the wheel. I pull back out onto Shea Boulevard. We pass through mountains suddenly. "You remember that it's Yom Kippur tomorrow?" my mother says.

"I forgot about it," I say.

"Well, you should say a prayer."

The fatigue and the sadness has me drunk, and the speed of the car in my hands feels good in a way that doesn't terrify for the first time in years. My mother closes her eyes, falls nearly asleep but still tells me to slow down as we drift into the town beyond the hills, its strange constellations of homes stretched between darkness.

BY MORNING, EVERYTHING WAS grey swept, the prickly brush swathed in rain. Inhaling the fumes of the storm, the greened soil, the sage, I knew beauty for me would only ever be derived from loss. I saw Sonora before me, so otherworldly, so desolate, some cast-out mistress on the pale blue planet, and longed suddenly to stay.

"I'll miss this," I said.

Laura said nothing and turned the car radio on. The rain had cooled the desert. We sang together. I screamed beside her, singing though I did not know the words. The entire desert still slept. One woman appeared with her dog, jogging in the first light. We approached the canal. The wash at its side was flooded. There was an ambulance parked on the banks.

"Slow down a second," Laura said.

Another ambulance rushed toward us. Laura undid her seat belt and stood up through the sunroof. "Looks like they're rescuing someone from the canal," she said drearily.

"When we first got here, my father and I used to walk right up to this side of the canal and feed coyotes at night," I said.

"Oh, where have all the coyotes gone to?" Laura crooned.

Laura and I drove through the sunrise, a sunrise gaudy in its fuchsia and indigo. In a few hours, everything would be cleaned up. The ambulance would disperse. The scene at the canal would gradually become as oblivious as the morning's clear sky.

Too many had died. It was against all statistical odds. I thought it was the landscape so lonely it pained us, so beautiful it urged us to accidental suicide. Atop the mountains that faced the old apartment complex was a radio tower. When I first saw it, I imagined it to be a signal that recovered the movements of aliens and spaceships, hovering over us, always waiting for the right moment to take us up and out.

IT'S DAWN BY THE time we park in the hospital. The storm never comes. I turn off the ignition. As if on cue, my mother and I both remain in the car.

"We were just a normal family, so normal that we had dinner together every night," my mother says. "Is this the right lot?"

"You already forgot?" I say.

"We should all take a trip somewhere," my mother says. "I need to see the ocean. I need to get out of here. You've been gone so long, you forget what it's like to live without seeing water."

IT ONLY TOOK A few hours for the heat to rise past a hundred and ten degrees. Everything was brittle and cracked. When I got home, I heard the sound of wood being dragged across the tile floor, the sound of struggling and banged glass. My father was cursing to himself in Arabic. Sharmut was whining, running back and forth through the hall as if chasing and then being chased by an invisible beast. My mother was hitting the table over and over again as if this might stop him.

I asked my father what he was doing. "We won't need this anymore," he screamed. His face was red, and his arms were already bruised from handling the weight.

He left the piano in the middle of the yard, the dead August grass sunken down around its legs. Shortly afterward, it began to rain again. My mother begged him to save the piano.

My father slammed the door to the garage and got into his car. "It's not about you, Rachel! She is spoiled, our daughter, and has to learn what happens when you give up your dreams. Dancing is for prostitutes. New York is for whores who stay out all night."

I covered myself up in a quilt. I was suddenly cold. My father returned. He stomped into the living room and pulled the television from the wall and then was out the door. "Out with the trash," he yelled. "You ready to go?"

"Where were you all night?" my mother asked.

"Somebody died," I said.

"Are you on drugs?"

We drove to the airport in my father's taxi. We were approaching the terminal when my father finally spoke. "I only had one friend in New York, a poet from my hometown. He was very famous. But we were refugees. Aliens. So it didn't matter I was nobody. I couldn't see him unless I brought him a bottle of vodka. He was the best poet alive, but he had his ways. Vodka or nothing. The last night I saw him, after we finished the bottle, I was going and he said to me, 'Yusef, New York will ruin you.' He said to me, 'It ruins everyone eventually.'"

"That's not true," my mother said.

"He burned to death that night. Left his cigarette going. Burned in his own apartment. No one came to save him. No one cared he was a famous poet. No one cared until the flames were in the hall. No one thought anything when they smelled smoke. That's New York for you."

My father unlocked the door and put the car into park. When I got out, he rolled down the window. "Always take a taxi, Ahlami."

My mother jumped out of the car. "This is yours now." It was the ring she wore always that I adored most, a gold band with three onyx stones.

I sat in the window seat of the airplane. Laura was next to me, her head on my shoulder. The voices spiraled through my mind like migrating sparrows. I had no brain. I was a segue for the birds to pass through. My head was full of them. I looked down at the desert disappearing through the clouds and squeezed my eyes shut.

I was outside in my parents' yard before the piano. I opened its sheath. The keys moved without me. The wind picked me up from beneath my armpits. I wanted to be back on the ground but couldn't. I tried to move, tried to dance, tried to land. The music was beautiful. I couldn't move my limbs. The keys, I saw from this height, were made of bones. Everything below me, the desert, a graveyard.

The music turned ugly. I couldn't do anything but rise, pinned like a cross by the wind. I was made of stars. The sky was thick, dull, grey, impenetrable.

I came to at the sound of my mother's voice calling my name. But there was only Laura there, humming a song I did not know. And then we were coming down.

⎯ᵧᵧᵧᵧ⎯

IT WAS BRIGHT AND cloudless as we flew over New York. From the plane I saw a hint of the skyline before we turned and passed over the Atlantic, then looped back toward the shore. We saw figures on the beach, figures in the waves. Boats were making their slow journey across the ocean. By the time we left the airport, the sky had turned a menacing grey. The rain made a clanking music on the subway tracks. Laura had insisted we take the train.

There were only a few people waiting. It seemed like such a quiet scene, almost abandoned. There was a man walking toward nowhere between the train tracks and a metal gate. Marsh consumed his path. Everything in the street below us was closed except a single bar named after the station. A seagull swooped down and landed on the platform. I could smell the ocean.

It did not conform to the vision of bustle and elegance

and light I associated with New York. A woman walked to the edge of the track and leaned over it. There was no train. She was dressed in all black. Her face was solemn, her eyes wet. She lit a cigarette.

"We're home," Laura said.

Finally the train arrived, creeping forth as if there were traffic ahead. Laura mocked the sound of the doors opening and closing. She did a cartwheel on the floor of the car and crashed into a seat, laughing.

I sat by the window watching the endless graves just beyond the A train's tracks while she studied the map. Then the train submerged. When the doors opened, I loved the smell. The musk of the underground—it was sordid, teeming with life. "Do you notice how no one is looking at anyone else?" Laura said. "It's amazing." She was pacing the length of the car pretending to read the ads.

"You're nervous about seeing him," I said.

"I know you are, but what am I?" she said in a childish voice, then frowned. "I can't figure out the map."

I had written out the directions on my palm. From delivering pizzas with her, I knew Laura had no talent for maps. She would take a left three turns too late, miss freeway exits, and then argue with the road as if it had changed overnight.

We switched to the F train, and after a few stops, the train suddenly bore itself up above Brooklyn. The skyline was before us. Those buildings at last so close were a magic trick, and in the last light, they glittered through the mist, regal and secretive. The emerald arm of the Statue of Liberty shot through the screen of rain. The Twin Towers cradled the moon between them before the clouds again disappeared half the sky. We were going in the opposite direction, though, toward a flattened land, factory smoke, graffiti scrawled on old warehouses. A canal. As we exited the train, a man begging for change boarded. His face had been burned off so badly the contours between nose and cheek and mouth were gone.

Only a few cars passed us. There was a bodega on the corner, an ancient sign on its exterior advertising cold beer, cigarettes, chips. Two men sat in lawn chairs at the train exit in front of the single brownstone on the street. They were covered by a large umbrella stand decorated with cacti. Before them was a large cardboard box of watermelons.

"Evening, sirs," Laura said.

They tipped their hats. From the looks of it, they were father and son. "Do you know where a Dylan lives?" Laura asked. They nodded us in the direction of the canal.

"Down there," the son said. "Then left."

As we crossed the street, the father called after us, "Careful now."

We turned off into an alley that ran along the canal and opened onto a large parking lot. There was the old Chevy

Dylan had driven us in years earlier in the center of the lot with its roof charred. Its bed was covered now by a tent. It was going nowhere ever again. The sound of the above-ground train screeched overhead, leaving us for its journey to the sea. A stray cat approached me, nestling against my leg. Shards of glass lay in a thick carpet on the asphalt. Mosquitoes swarmed from puddles. A large boulder painted purple with an X sat in front of the door atop a rain-worn American flag. Dylan had written there: *So beautiful, we have built the crucifix on which we hang.*

"Did you get lost?" Dylan said. He crawled out of the tent on the truck and walked toward us. He was taller and thinner than when he left. His hair had strands of grey. His presence suddenly made things feel off-kilter, gorgeous as if being crushed in lush velvet while cascading off the edge of a cliff.

"It's beautiful here," Laura said.

"Well, here we are again," he said and looked around as if he too had only just arrived. "Let's go in?"

I had never seen such large windows. Every change of the sky was painted before us. The trains passed, and their lights swept into the loft. Inside it smelled like a leftover fire and dirty laundry. Chandeliers were sprawled across the ceiling like a canopy of trees, their bulbs blue. There was a single bed in the middle of it all like a stage. Shattered mirrors hung from the walls in place of decoration. Dylan had written phrases all over his walls in various colors of spray paint: *abandoned altars, apocalypse tango, we, the pretty fallen angels, alchemy: shit = gold, garbage truck booty call, the oceans of Europa, midnight in the Y2K,* and a nod to us, perhaps: *the Phoenix Lights.*

The entire space was filled with broken instruments. There were three out-of-tune pianos and four guitars that were missing strings. An accordion lay out of its case on the window ledge. Dylan opened three beers with a lighter and handed them to us. He took up one of the guitars and began to restring it. "Won't you play something for us, Laura?" he said.

"If she dances," Laura said, looking at me.

Dylan finished his beer and walked out the door into the lot. We heard the glass crash against the concrete. "Therapy," he said when he returned.

Laura began fiddling with the guitar, touching a string, winding the bolts on the head to tune. "Give it to me," Dylan said. "I'll play. You sing. Ahlam dances."

"It's Ariel," I said. Dylan looked at me ironically.

"I prefer Ahlam" he said. "More exotic."

He played a dark, repetitive tune, vaguely oriental. He did not look at us, just down at the instrument, swaying his head, his eyes fluttering shut. Laura hummed lowly at first, looking at me angrily to fulfill my role in the trance of our first night. She pulled me to her. We spun around each other, laughing. I chaînéd from her swiftly and bowed.

She rubbed her legs with her hands as if trying to clean them and then began to sing "La Llorona" to the tune of Dylan's playing. She howled the song, louder than I'd ever heard her, conjuring all angels and all devils, her young voice husky and ancient, and as she did, I watched Dylan watching her, his gaze fixed on the new exceptional animal occupying his home. Then he looked at me.

"Your friend is going to be a star," he said. "Let's go make a fire."

Dylan began picking up pieces of wood. A cat hissed at him, its tail growing large, its eyes red, and ran toward the canal. "You know," he said, "I had this uncle on my mother's side. Well, my uncle never slept. He'd go out to the bar for three days in a row, leaving my aunts and cousins in the house. He spent days drinking and would come home finally, maybe on the third or fourth day, having not slept, and he'd sit up all night for another seven days drinking vodka and making fire after fire after fire in the yard, winter or summer, until his wife came out and screamed at him to put it out, but he couldn't hear her. It was like he was in a trance. He didn't speak or sleep."

"That's a strange story," I said.

"That's who I come from. Strange people. So how long are you ladies planning to be in New York?"

"We come from even stranger people than you," Laura said.

"Maybe a year?" I said.

Dylan walked toward me. "Can I see this?" he asked. Before I could answer, he slipped my mother's ring off me, and fit as much as he could onto his blistered and bruised finger. "What a pretty thing this is," he said. "But it's not black diamond. And what are you doing here in New York? What are you looking for?" Without waiting for my answer, he slipped off the ring. "Now we are forever connected."

"We're escaping hell," Laura said. She looked hurt by the brief redirection of attention.

"When I met you girls," Dylan said, "I thought I had a demon in me. I wanted to live with the Hopis in the high desert. That's why I left you guys so abruptly." Dylan blew on the flames, making the fire go. "But they wouldn't even talk to me. I drove all the way up there to the high desert and pleaded with them to just tell me something, anything. Someone I knew had died and . . . well, they just looked at me like I was speaking another language. Finally one of the kids walked up to me. I thought I had finally broken through."

"Had you?" Laura said.

"The kid told me I was an asshole." Dylan laughed. "So I came back here. That's the good thing about New York. It never rejects the impure. In fact, it does the opposite."

"I'm trying to be a dancer," I said. "To return to your earlier question."

"And she's *so* pure about it," Laura said.

"Trying?" he said. "You either are or you aren't. Never say 'trying to be' in this city. You'll end up a drug-addicted failure. Trust me. Always say 'I am' even if you don't believe it yourself."

Wind blew the fire toward the canal, extinguishing most of it. Laura took up the ax to split another log.

Dylan halted her with his arm. "Tonight you ladies take the bed. I'll sleep in the truck."

I woke up to the sound of the trains passing over us every few minutes. Laura was still snoring. Dylan was sitting at the piano with a beer. The sheath was closed, but he was moving his head like some mad conductor.

"I think it was Van Gogh who said the only cure for suicide was to breakfast on a glass of beer and a slice of bread," he said.

"I barely slept," I said.

"Oh, you must be a normal person," he said. "One of those people who thinks they need sleep."

⸏⸏⸏⸏

MY MOTHER AND I sleep on either side of my father. I do not know what we will do when it will be just the two of us. Will she still want to shop? Will I still smoke so much?

It's morning in the hospital. I hear the nurses chatter, the heightened frequency of footsteps in the hall. Phones are ringing. Televisions are turned on. I wake up but know that the room is still full of ghosts. Everything whispers. The way voices sound in an old bar, the music turned off, the night ripped from them by morning. I was kissed in one dream. I was running up a flight of steps that went on forever, looking for someone who would die if I didn't make it to the top in time.

I catch the reflection of my face in the steel sink. I stand up and hold my father's hand. His eyes open. "I'm alive?" he asks.

ON THE CORNER OF our street, near the watermelon men, was a single brownstone and a sign in its yard that read, MEMBERS ONLY. Our first morning, Dylan peeked in and asked for the special. He exchanged hugs and handshakes with everyone there. We were not introduced. He emerged with three beers, though it was noon, and three plates of eggy grits and shrimp. "Eat quick. I have to be in the city by one."

When we emerged from the subway, I saw it, my New York. The one I had dreamed of all those years. The blocks were full, the streets dotted with yellow taxis. We were bombarded by sirens in every direction. I smelled the warm nuts and the hot dogs grilling and the smolder of the trains going and going beneath us. Everyone honked. The buildings glittered in the sun. The trash cans were brimming. Some blocks smelled of rotting fish, some of the cologne of clothing stores wafting into the street. On every corner hundreds of posters advertised concerts, parties, call girls. It was loud as a drug, and it made my mind quiet.

Dylan wandered into a restaurant. "Need a drink," he said and sat down at the bar. The waitress wore a bowler hat. She didn't smile at us. She looked askance as if there was some very interesting scene playing out in the restaurant just beyond us. We ordered orange juice. Dylan asked the waitress to add some champagne to his.

Dylan drank fast, always. Within moments, he put cash on the bar without seeing the check. "*Vámanos.*"

"You're such an alcoholic," Laura said.

"Indeed I am, Laura. But I'm also so much more than that."

Dylan did not tell us where we were going. He walked fast, half a block ahead of us. I read the time at the top of a building: it was seventeen minutes past one. We were already late. The elevator opened up directly into an apartment. One of Dylan's chandeliers hung in the entryway. There was a single white leather couch, bar stools. Everything smelled new, like money.

"These are my art assistants," Dylan said as we entered. "They're doing an internship with me."

"Lovely to meet you," the hostess said. I knew she was about the age of my mother, but her thinness and her crisp dress and the way her nails were painted and her hair coiffed told me she was nothing like my mother, that she could have whatever she wanted. We sat quietly as she spoke to Dylan over glasses of white wine and small sandwiches, her hand occasionally resting on his shoulder a few minutes too long. They were speaking about people we'd never heard of with calibrated passion. Laura began to fidget.

The hostess turned to us. "Do you two study art? Are you in college now?"

"Yes," Dylan said. "They are students."

"So you're old enough to drink, then?" She laughed.

"Yeah, of course," Laura said.

"I'm a dancer too," I said.

The hostess snuck a glance at her watch while sipping her wine. It was still three quarters full. Ours were already empty. "I feel like I've seen you somewhere before," she said to Laura. "Do you model?"

"No, but everyone asks me that," she said.

"You have such an exquisite face," the hostess said.

I was drunk by the time Dylan hailed us a cab. He shouted directions at the driver, his foot perched on the console. Laura sat between us, her head on my shoulder, her skirt hitched up so that her thighs directly touched Dylan's jeans.

Wherever we ended up, we stayed through the night. Dylan left us alone and wandered the crowd. A band came on and played, and then another. I had fallen asleep in a booth when Laura shook me. "We're going to a party."

"Another?" I asked.

We walked some blocks, the haze of light and noise like a dream. I was stumbling, my arms around Laura for support, Dylan just ahead of us. Finally we approached a red door and went up some stairs to an apartment. There were six people there when we arrived, but throughout the night, the buzzer rang and more and more flooded in. Someone passed around a plate of cocaine, someone passed around a joint. Laura sucked on the marijuana. Finally there was a crowd around the couch listening to an older man play the guitar. He was slurring the lyrics of the songs, tilting from his stool.

"Why don't you play?" Dylan said to Laura. "He's a very important producer, you know."

"I'm shy," she said.

"Stop that," he said and pulled the skin at her cheek.

Everyone was still talking as Laura began to sing, and then the chatter grew dimmer and dimmer, and then the chatter was gone. The entire party was watching her. My face grew hot. She sang a song, slowly and quietly and then louder and more violently until I was back in the desert with her, the bushes shivering, the mountains shaking. When she was finished, the older man who had been playing banged his beer down on the table. "Now that's a damn fine voice. Where have I seen you play at little girl? Knitting Factory? Limelight?"

"Yes, Limelight," Laura said, smiling from inside her lie. Her shirt had slipped off her shoulder, exposing the scar she had until then always immediately covered up.

That night, waiting sleeplessly into the dawn for Laura to come in from the truck, I watched the first bustle of trains pass overhead. It was near night again when I awoke to her beside me. She was talking in her sleep.

Laura and I got jobs as waitresses at a pizzeria three blocks from Dylan's. He'd agreed we could stay with him until we could afford a room elsewhere.

Laura forgot to light the candles on the tables. She missed appetizers and drinks in her customers' orders. She left bits of cork floating in the wine. She was fired after her first weekend. "Whatever," she said. "Dylan's friend got me a show in September."

I traveled into the city for ballet classes. I didn't make any friends. Most of the dancers were older than me and back in school. Most were trying to be nurses and librarians and some were trying to be actresses. None were still trying to be ballerinas. Most were better than I was. I was imprecise, my turnout, my pointe, was not well articulated. Where had I trained, the teachers wanted to know. But I was still young. There was time, they said.

One ballerina dined in the restaurant daily and alone. She ordered garden salads or broth. A club soda. Never a single slice of pizza. Beneath the table, she moved her feet from second position to third and fourth and fifth. We never spoke until one night I served her cocktails with her meal. "Don't let it ruin you," I heard her say as I walked away. I wanted to believe I had no idea what she was talking about. I wanted to believe I had forgotten everything my father had ever said.

In the weeks leading up to Laura's show, Dylan and Laura went to parties where she met booking managers, producers, writers, gallerists, directors, actors, filmmakers. I was always missing something while on shift. Labor Day had come and gone, and it was the first September in my life that I had not returned to school. The air changed immediately and cooled. The leaves in the new wind made a shivery melody on my path home, almost already yellow in the late summer sun.

I walked the city often. When I came home too late and Laura and Dylan were already gone, I took the train with a notebook and rode it to the end of the line all the way out to Coney Island. On the subway, I wrote choreography inspired by the city, my small body converged on by forces larger than monsoons, larger than mountains. Sometimes I switched lines and exited at Lincoln Center just to watch dancers pass me by, hoping one might recognize me there, praying one might notice I was meant to be among them. The past had been deleted in the struggle of the trains, the pushiness of the crowds, the loudness of the sirens, the music blasting in the street, all of it filled me up.

I had no visions. I had been excavated by the constant stimulation. The city blurred me, made me another of its anonymous spectators. I felt happiest in my exchanges at bodegas over the purchase of a coffee or cigarettes or when observing the break-dancers twirl and the mariachis croon. All intimacy was exchanged as if in a foreign language, via gestures and quick, mistaken glances on the train.

I wanted everything to remain like this, veiled in invisibility. I was afraid to meet a man, to sleep with a man. I believed in the suspicion that if I remained alone, untouched, the curse would not come for New York. No one would ever die again.

Finally, one night, I came home only to Laura. We had hardly been alone together. She was in the kitchen with a cello. Her legs were spread around it, and she was playing a more violent melody than I'd ever heard her play, banging the wood of the instrument like a hollow drum, destroying whatever pretty noise might come out.

"Where'd you get that?" I asked.

"Friend of Dylan's," she said and continued her banging between dissonant, awful chords.

"Why make it so ugly? Doesn't sound like your stuff."

"I'm evolving, Ariel," she said. "Can I get a smoke?"

"Where's your boyfriend?"

"He's my *lover*," she said. "And he happens to be out with another woman tonight." Laura lit her cigarette and pushed the cello toward me. "Don't look at me like that. We're not in Kansas anymore."

My FATHER TURNS TO me. "I love you more than anything, habibti. Have you been here with me all night?"

"Yes, Daddy," I say.

"Why do you look so serious?" he asks. "Smile a little. Take the hair out of your face. You are still a child. Do you know that I was thrown into the sea off the coast of Italy because I had no papers? My daughter should be happy. Go sit at the piano and play."

"We're in a hospital, Dad," I say.

"You know, I used to listen to you play. I would sneak in from the garage and listen to you. You didn't know it. Even when you made a mistake, I would smile. You don't know how beautiful you were."

LAURA'S SHOW CAME SO close to the beginning of everything. We had only just arrived. It was simple then to think life could change after only a night. We were eighteen and said we were twenty-three. I will be forever twenty-three. We must have looked so young. Our faces without wrinkle, fresh, our eyes unlocked. I see girls now at our age then, their posture high, their faces unwittingly too open, unbroken.

The bar was in the Lower East Side, and the bathrooms were unisex, the floors wet with toilet paper and used condoms, the walls filled with love letters and hate letters to the government. Dylan and I sat on stools near the bar toward the back and watched as the crowd poured in, all dressed in black with dyed hair everywhere, spiked chokers, and fishnet tights. He passed me a drink in a red plastic cup, and I almost vomited at the first sip.

"How you doing, white swan?" he shouted over the din.

"It's the same dancer," I said. "The black one and the white one."

"And who's your charming prince?" he asked.

A girl in a miniskirt nudged herself between us and ordered a drink. I watched Dylan's eyes on her body, tracing her curves. She bumped into me as she pushed back out into the crowd. Dylan pushed my hair behind my ear. "Bitch," he mouthed.

Laura began to play. She started soft, and the crowd screamed for her to sing louder. Her head whipped around, and she began banging the cello. Her voice croaked. "She's a natural," Dylan said. He was smoking, looking toward the stage at her, tapping his feet, his hand on my thigh casually at first, then rubbing through my jeans up and up, never looking back at me at all as if this were the way things always were for us.

The nausea in my stomach from the drink raced up into my throat. I ran to the bathroom and remained there through the rest of the show, through the applause, and through her finale, playing a mournful song the crowd at last allowed her. "Kol Nidre." I knew it was for me.

I left without them.

I walked as fast as I could toward the bridge. Everyone was drunk, walking aslant and stumbling. I brushed by them, chain-smoking. I crossed a street against the light when suddenly I heard a scream. I looked up, and a body was falling. At first glance, I believed it was a bag or a bird. I heard nothing of the man, only the pavement. The scream came from a woman leaning out her window.

The blood flowed fast and then stopped. The man was wearing a tuxedo, but his bow tie was missing, his shirt unbuttoned to his chest, his cuffs folded up. He was on the younger side of middle-aged. His eyes were open, blue. A child's eyes. A cop came running toward the scene from nowhere and blocked me off with his arm.

I backed away and began to run until I was on the ramp of the Williamsburg Bridge. I sat at its center, rocking to the rhythm of the rumbling train at my side, the cars passing, the boats blowing their horns beneath me as they passed over the river, their lights creating stars on the waves. A single man in orthodox dress passed me hurriedly, said nothing. I hadn't yet noticed how arrogant New York was, all of its cement and its lights and its suspension pulleys.

I heard the suited man hitting the pavement and knew that sound would be the same for a body hitting the river if the bridge caved through. On a mountain, your feet feel centuries of earth beneath them, the ground soft.

I closed my eyes and opened them and closed them and opened them, and the bridge was underwater, and where the cars and trains had been were now planes falling to the bottom of the depths toward watery graves. The man in the suit multiplied and fractured, like small crows crashing, falling farther through the riverbed.

I walked the entire way home, a small speck beside the river, the monumental city and all its flashy secrets, all its dazzling shows, at my side, through the brownstone streets where the wind was making a great commotion of the trees, all the while believing that the man was an omen of an end, the end of Laura and me. I would have to leave because of Dylan. She would become famous, and we would see each other for lunches or while home for the holidays. I would dance or I would not dance, and I would be greeted warmly by her after her shows as her old dear friend. It had already happened for her, everything she wanted. Our past would dissolve. We would move on from each other and from the ghosts of our youth. I would now just be the girl who'd followed her through the desert as a child. But she would always be my Laura, hanging from the cactus, weeping as the monsoon came for us both.

—×—×—×—

MY MOTHER STIRS AT the sound of our voices. She takes my father's hand in hers, then frowns.

"You're burning."

"Where have you put me? Why am I here?" he cries.

"You had surgery, Dad," I say. "Don't you remember it?"

He begins to shake, his legs, his arms. His teeth chatter. He pulls out one of the IVs from his arms. His eyes grow large as a prey before a predator. I can see the hair on his arms, goosebumps forming everywhere. He rises up to sit. "What is this?" he says, touching his gown. "Have you put me in a madhouse?"

"Calm down, Yusef." My mother moves toward the door. "I'll get the nurse."

"What nurse?" he screams. He looks toward me and grabs my arm. "I don't want a nurse. I want to go home!"

———

WE WERE ALL THREE of us still asleep when the plane hit the first tower. The sudden sirens everywhere at once brought me up and out and into the lot when I saw the black smoke pluming forth from the city. Laura's foot was sticking out of the tent, shaking in her sleep. I grabbed her leg and pulled, took her blanket and covered us beneath it as if this might save us, as if we could hide.

The drone of helicopters rushed overhead. Dylan was naked but ran out of the truck anyway and climbed the ladder to the roof. Laura had fallen to her knees by the time the second plane hit. Dylan walked toward the ledge and shouted at the men with the watermelons, "What the fucking fuck fuck," in a slur. Their box had spilled into the street.

I shut my eyes. *My father and I are walking in the desert.*

But the desert is too long. When does the desert end? I heard his voice. "Laura," I said. My eyes would not shut. The dust was already out to sea, already coming for us, already covering us.

V

FEBRUARY

THERE WERE NO CONCERTS, no gallery openings, no parties. There were no nights stomping maudlin across the bridge home, taking taxis, the breeze in our hair, gazing at the lights of the city rushing away from us and all its promises, all its power. I saw no ballerinas; Laura left the instruments in their cases. All shows were canceled. We stayed at Dylan's.

We edged toward winter, and day by day, New York grew dark earlier. The leaves were thick in the streets. The first snow fell. Leaving the subway late at night was not as scary as it was lonely in the cold. The wind from the river blew so hard I lost my footing. The train swayed. The old Kentile Floors factory sign kept watch over us, a remnant of the defunct industrial past. So long bereft of any use, we thought it beautiful solely for the fact that it endured when everything else had changed. We watched the flakes melt into the black canal, as if in a hurry to flee their swirl, become sludge.

People have always needed somewhere new to go and quick when old things disappear, and it was perhaps for this that they began to gather at Dylan's. It was slow at first, friends stopping in for drinks that lasted late into the night on any given day. But then it became every night that I would find someone or other lying on my bed, sprawled in a daze of booze and marijuana. Someone in a corner, all pale, speaking to no one in particular about what had happened, all the conspiracies already, this was all for Israel, it was Israel's fault, calling Dylan's corner at the end of everything, paradise, nothing could touch us there, reading his scrawl, thinking it scripture. And there were always girls, girls in chokers, girls with magenta hair, girls with guitars, girls carrying canvases, girls who had lost someone in the attacks, girls who liked girls and boys, girls who ended up crying about the fucked-up world and remained with us in the morning, always, always staying in the tent in the truck in the lot.

But the first official party did not happen until the New Year. Dylan hung a swing from the ceiling he had made of a plank of wood and rope, and set up pillows in the old window-less freight elevator that smelled of urine so people could ride up and down, drunk or high, like some sick circus ride. "Like passing through the rings of hell," he said.

Before anyone had even arrived, he had set out a bowl of

cocaine in the center, surrounded by bottles of vodka, tequila, gin. Beside the coke was a stack of blades he used for cutting paper and two sheets of glass with a pressed lily between them. "¿*Qué es?*" Laura asked.

"The white blossom," he said.

The fractured mirrors surrounded us, the bed, the swing, the table, as in some carnival funhouse, reflecting us back to ourselves, our fissure, what we were becoming. The lot grew full of people we did not know shattering beer bottles off the concrete walls as Dylan had urged them to do, howling at their capacity for destruction, expressing admiration at how good they could smash up their pain. Dylan had set up a station for lighting fireworks over the canal.

It became a trend that after women took lines of cocaine, they would kiss each other provocatively for the camera. There was always someone taking pictures. I had never until that night tried the stuff.

"Just do a line. You won't die or anything, promise," Laura said.

Dylan was suddenly behind us, his arms around our bodies, his breath hot on my shoulder. He could be so becoming, even with vodka on his breath. He took a key from his pocket and scooped some powder onto it. He held it to Laura's nostril, and then to mine.

"Dance with me," Laura said. Her hand was reaching for Dylan's, but he shrugged her off. He took the camera away from the photographer.

"Come here, then," she said to me. "Sit on my lap." Laura pulled me onto the swing. "Here," she said. "You've got glitter on your lips."

Her lips were soft, her tongue softer than any boy's. It curled around mine, probing. I hadn't been kissed since Eli. Her hands went to my neck. My bones shuddered. I was her marionette. I was her dancer; she was my music. Her hair brushed my shoulder. We paused, and our lips joined again. Her breath tasted of wine. I felt the cocaine burn in my throat.

She drew away. When I looked up, Dylan was watching us, the camera at his side. Laura bounced off the swing. She had won him for the night.

In the morning, we heard that thousands of birds had fallen from the sky in cities all over the world. Fish had washed up on shores across the country, their blood staining the beaches on that first day of the year. I had believed if I touched no one, no one would die. If I skipped the cracks, if I saw nothing, if we were out of the desert, we had escaped hell—but it wasn't true. Everything was just dying faster in the world.

———

THE NURSE SWEEPS INTO the room. She ignores my mother and me. My mother's legs are crossed; her hands are on her temples. I know she is getting a migraine. "You have a fever," the nurse says to my father. "I'll get the doctor."

"I'm happy with a fever; a fever I can handle. As long as I can walk without pain," he says.

"What does that mean?" my mother shrieks. "Why would he have a fever?"

"Mom, calm down," I say.

"Calm down, Rachel," my father says.

"It's relatively common. A bad reaction to the anesthesia," the nurse says and leaves us.

"When can I go home?" my father calls after her. He sits up in the bed. My mother leans over him to wrestle him down. "You can't make me stay here!" he screams.

———

THE SNOW TURNED THE nights violet. On the subway, I knew warmth from huddling against strangers in the crowded train. On the coldest nights, Laura and Dylan slept inside. We had one industrial heater that worked intermittently. I could smell Dylan, though Laura lay between us. And for knowing it was his smell, for taking note of it at all, I felt guilty. When we were all together, he never tried to touch me, and though I had seen him naked a dozen times by then, he slept in the bed inside with his jeans and boots on. Some nights he never came home at all, and it was just Laura and me. If I tried to speak of where he might be, she changed the subject or left me alone to smoke a cigarette by the canal. There were subjects we suddenly no longer touched like an old married couple making do.

One night, there were sirens and a crowd of people staring into the canal. The bridge was covered in ice. The snow heaved into us with the wind, sputtering out over the canal like confetti. In the water below, we saw a dolphin, perking its head in and out of the water, its face and skin covered in the black liquid poison that filled the canal.

"He's crying," Laura said.

"He must have gotten lost coming in from the ocean," said one of the bystanders. "They're going to let him die here."

"Can't someone get in and save him?" Laura said.

"No one is going in there," the woman said.

"No one is going to save him?" Laura screamed.

That night, we were alone, and I awoke to Laura's naked back, the sprawl of freckles on her browned skin reminding me in the confused half-light of waking next to the one back I'd loved before. I covered her up. How she did not wake from the cold, I still do not know. She always spoke in her sleep, sometimes in Spanish, sometimes in English, sometimes in a language I did not recognize. She was always thin, and thinner that winter. Her ribs were like an accordion beneath her skin. Her legs shook in her sleep.

I couldn't sleep and walked to the kitchen. I looked at the clock. It was only still evening in Arizona. I dialed my father for the first time. In the past months, I had only spoken to my mother.

He did not say hello, only, "Are you ready to come home?"

"I am trying to dance," I said.

"No, you want to ruin your life," he said. "And die there while you're at it."

"Dad, please."

"'Please' is not going to help you. I had a dream last night that you've been given the evil eye."

"I just wanted to say—" I began.

"Come home," he interrupted me, then hung up.

I smoked a cigarette by the window and watched the trains crisscross, stall, and then slowly dip underground again. I walked back to the bed. On the nightstand was a leather-bound journal. I whispered, "Laura" to see if she was awake. She snored once and turned over. I opened the book.

There was sheet music pasted in, drawings of Dylan, a photo of the two of us young on the steps of my old apartment building, looking ironic or bored, the desert behind us. There was a letter penned in nice script, in Spanish, signed *Maria*. The letter was old and yellowing. Below in Laura's own hand, I read, *the curse must be broken*. And below that, *a Jonah of the desert*. The rest of the pages were blank except for a single photo in the back.

I noticed Laura staring at me and flipped the book closed.

Dylan walked in at that moment and destroyed whatever angry exchange there might have been.

"I was stuck in a train for three hours," he said. "People were going mad, trying to climb out the windows into the tunnel. They didn't tell us anything, just kept us like that. For three fucking hours." He walked toward the bed and lifted the covers off us. "Did you hear me?"

"*Sí, jefe,*" Laura said. I pretended to be asleep.

"Get me a beer," he said and slapped her leg. "And you . . . sleep outside with Laura. I want to be alone in my own home."

In the tent, I woke up sick with a fever. It was pure fever without vision or chorus of voices. I slept the entire day. I remembered none of it except for one dream of my mother. I saw my mother's face as an adult's, her body that of a child. I spoke to her, but she would not acknowledge me. She sat before a wall of indigo glass vases and, just beyond it, the Galilee.

Outside the window where the vases were shelved, the olive trees wrapped tortuously about everything. There were gardens of azalea, white roses, walls laced with bougainvillea. We walked through the garden, my mother and I, without saying a word. The fountain was covered over with moss. Everything reeked of disintegration. We arrived at the lake, at the Sea of Galilee. We stood there and watched as its surface changed, turned into the canal just beside Dylan's, full of abandon, full of rot. The late afternoon turned to night. We looked up and over the lake, stars fell. My mother looked at me. She was trying to tell me something, but her mouth would not open.

When the fever broke, Laura was sitting beside me,

smoking. The sunlight through the flap of the tent was so cold it was blue. The sheets were wet beneath me. She had covered me in her mother's coyote fur. "I sang for you."

"How can you love him?" I said.

"You know how," she said.

Dylan had not sold a piece of art the entire time we lived there, so when he finally did, for a healthy five figures, he told us, there was another party. It was bigger than the last. There were a DJ and burlesque dancers, the elevator was outfitted in disco lights, and there was a small canoe in the canal so guests could row out over the waste. Hundreds of people came in eclectic costumes. Dylan walked among his guests like a king. Everyone knew his name. The old producer smashed Dom Pérignon bottles against the wall and then sat on the swing with a girl who had her hair in pigtails. Laura shouted at him that the swing would break, and he looked at her as if he'd never known her at all.

There was a dancer climbing a piece of fabric suspended from the ceiling. She flew. We drank absinthe, we drank champagne. I was dizzy. I was swaying. The din was deafening. Suddenly Laura was nowhere, and Dylan was behind me, his hand at my hip. "Come here. Come with me," he whispered. I followed him to the bathroom.

He had a vial in one hand. He poured it out on the toilet seat. "You look a little overwhelmed," he said. "Maybe this will help."

"I'm good," I said.

He took two lines off the porcelain and poured the powder on the indent between his thumb and forefinger. He pushed my face, softly, down into his hand. I sniffed. He spit into his fingers and pushed through my jeans into my underwear. "I don't want you to feel good. I want you to swim in fucking starlight."

I slammed the bathroom door. Laura was in the kitchen taking shots. No one had seen. Nothing had happened.

And then I wasn't swaying. And then I was dancing inside the crowd. And then I was in love with every man and woman whose sweat touched mine. I was lying down, my head in the lap of a beautiful stranger, who caressed my hair, my arms, his eyes bright, concerned. "Who are you?"

"I'm a dancer," I said.

"That's pretty, a dancer," he said. "Pretty, pretty dancer dancing in the desert. Pretty warrior dancer. But who is going to save Sonora?"

Laura shook me. I had fallen asleep outside on the bench beside the fire.

"Where'd he go?" I cried.

"Where'd who go?" she said. "Who were you dreaming of, Sleeping Beauty?"

The sun was up. The last embers were dying in the firepit. There were only a few of us left. Some were drinking beside the canal, unable to let the party end. Wishing it to go on. Cursing the last guest for leaving. And then, from hundreds, there were only just we three, as if there was never a party at all.

Where we lived, there were no bars, no restaurants, no flea markets. Only the bodega and the train station, the men and their watermelon stand at their own parties in the *members only* club raging on, undisturbed. We liked to say we were in the middle of the desert, the end of the world.

I'd walk in the middle of the street to remain visible to the little traffic there was. Every night, I'd pass the woman who sat on the drawbridge over the canal. She would pull down her pants in front of the few passersby and police. In the afternoons she would punch the air and in the early mornings would scream at someone certainly still locked up with her inside her mind. "You come from a sick house, a sick family."

During her monologues she would lapse into a maniacal clapping, her accent sometimes British and of another era, sometimes of the American street. "You destroyed my life!" she bellowed over the canal. Sometimes she would relieve herself in the polluted marsh at its banks. When she was finished, she'd speak of her actions in the third person. "Can you believe that bitch just took a shit?"

She always wore the same thing: black leggings and a sweatshirt wrapped around her head like a turban. I never knew where she showered or slept. She never asked for anything. I never asked her name. I thought sometimes she was a creature born of that polluted waterway, the Gowanus, stinking worse than feces in the unbearable summers, a conglomerate character of its strange beauty by moonlight and boastful wreckage by daylight.

One particularly freezing night, three police officers surrounded her and told me to walk on the other side of the street. I heard her call to me for the first time. "Tell them you are seeing this. Help me."

This, we were told, was part of the city cleaning up.

MY MOTHER YELLS AT the nurse, "Why is the doctor taking so long?" and then collapses into a fit of coughing. The sound hurts even me. I take my father's hand. He escapes the grasp of the nurse and shoves me off. He tries to stand but is too weak.

"We're going to have to restrain him," the nurse says. "He has to calm down."

My father falls silent. He lies back down. And this is almost worse. I cannot look into his eyes. They are lopsided, mahogany. I cannot look at him in this bed. I stare out the window, stare out into the desert. My eyes glaze over. I wish for the doctor, for a scream, a siren, to break the silence. Break what we feel, being in this room, relying on machines to measure the life coursing in us, measuring the beats we have left.

"Did you dream, Daddy?" I ask. He looks at me fearfully. "While you were out?"

"Ocean," he says. "And I wanted to swim. So I did. But the waves were strong. At the top of the beach, there were houses. But between the sand and the houses, there was a drop. A cliff. There were people living in the cliff with candles, praying. And there were people at the bottom of the cliff. People who didn't survive being thrown back from the ocean. I thought that was where I was going. The ocean was throwing me back so hard I'd miss the beach and fall into that cliff."

My father begins to cry. The salt is in my throat, my mouth.

"Which ocean was it?" I ask.

"Home," he says.

THAT WINTER, LAURA AND I took the train to the Atlantic Ocean. We stood on the boardwalk, pieces of snow in our hair. The ocean was darker than I imagined, far darker than the clear sea in Mexico. It was so loud. Planes flew overhead. The waves tumbled violently. The beach was empty except for three Orthodox Jews, all in black, walking beneath large umbrellas. "Looks like a funeral," Laura said.

"Is it any better here?" I said.

"Where do you think that plane is going? Maybe we should go there."

"Paris," I said.

"*Oui, oui,*" she said in an exaggerated French accent. "*Mademoiselle, venez ici, vous êtes très jolie.*"

"I'm cold," I said.

"Even the fucking sun is cold here." She pulled at her hair, stretching, squinting toward the horizon, though it was overcast. "The thing about New York is that it's unavoidable. Maybe that is the only way to be, the sort of person no one can consider forgetting. Like Dylan. You have to be hated and loved by everyone at the same time to accomplish that."

"So I should just go on as blow job girl forever."

"Yes," she said. Her face lightened. "That's a great idea."

The men with their black umbrellas turned uphill on the sand from the water. They walked in single file, the eldest leading the younger men behind him. They all had cigarettes. As they passed Laura and me, they averted their gaze. Laura called, "Hello." The youngest nodded. They walked down the beach and then paused. They wrapped their arms in Tefillin, then took a few steps forward and back and began to rock. The ocean muffled their words.

"Looks like they are praying to the ocean," Laura said.

"This city needs a prayer," I said. "But they're looking at Jerusalem."

"We need a fucking prayer."

At Dylan's, some days I woke up to white noise blaring from the television though the house was empty.

In the shower, I heard someone at the piano. A short

melody that drifted or a single note banged on as a child will play, delighted at the violent sounds they can make, not worried for the instrument, not knowing it to be one of the few things left reserved only for beauty. Then the sheath slammed shut. The instruments were all half desired, half forgotten. It was as if they were left behind by a ghost right in the middle of playing.

Sometimes in the corner of my eye, I saw a girl running through the loft. A see-through girl, a silhouette. She looked the way the world looks without my glasses. Vaguely hued, indistinct. She looked the way a body looks underwater, lost in the blur of bubble and wave.

I sat beside the window and imagined the view of the Gowanus Canal was the canal in Arizona beside which my father and I used to walk. A desert canal snaking through the city. I imagined it blue and full of swimmers. I imagined it sunlit. I imagined saguaro in place of signs, paloverde instead of cars. I saw the buildings melt to mountains. Like hunting for a dead beloved's face among the living, in places, we find the place we loved before. Now here was New York, torn through by dust.

I understood why someone would look at the ocean only to be in the direction of Jerusalem. I understood Bedouins who created odes to lovers lost in abandoned camps, lovers who would never be seen again. I understood it in my bones. Longing made the music bigger. Sometimes the sound of someone playing a Bach Partita on their violin wafted out into the winter streets, and I closed my eyes and imagined I was walking through a storm in the desert. Sometimes at work I heard my voice change, I heard Laura in the way I talked, a certain phrase, a certain grammatical error, her favorite conjunction that never existed, *and-or-else, and-or-else we'll just live by the sea*, felt her in the way that I moved, how over the years I came to light my cigarettes just like her, between ring and middle fingers, how I laughed or how my cash was always stuffed and disorganized in my wallet, just like hers was. I had brought her into my skin. I dreamed sometimes that in the mirror was her face reflected back at me. Still, I don't know where she ended and I began.

I never took anyone home. After seven years, I told myself, my cells would be entirely different. I have always been susceptible to a fool's suspicions. Walking on cracks, the myth of renascence after a set of years, but somehow I ignored all of Dylan's broken mirrors. When seven years had passed after Eli, I would find a man and we would make love and we would cross the ocean, live entirely elsewhere of everything.

But there were still men everywhere. And there was power in being so young. I barely knew how to wear my own face. But I was nothing desperate, hardly aware of time being a thing that might affect the eyes, the hair, the legs.

One night I met a Frenchman. His suit smelled expensive. I sat alone with him over six cocktails. He wore a Cartier watch. He spoke to me in French, blew in my ears, kissed my palms with the slightest tongue, warmed my calf with his hand. His eyes were a soft blue. His cologne was already on my skin.

"I live downtown," he said at last.

He hailed a cab for us. In the backseat, we kissed. His hands were already in my skirt. His suit buttons opened onto his chest. He opened the car door for me, exited, and paid the driver from the window of the passenger seat. I looked out upon it, Ground Zero. The American flag was still in the windless night. The shreds of buildings in heaps. Police cars lined the perimeter. The glow of rescue lights flowed across the scene, fogged in the dust that had not settled. Everything smelled of a fire gone wrong. All the hair of the centuries burned off the dead. I slammed the door and told the cabbie my address. The Frenchman banged on the back of the car as we drove away. Still, I wonder about him.

I found Laura that night lying down on the floor in the center of the loft with all of the chandeliers off but one, glowing atop her so that she was made of blue. Her arms spread open. I noticed a new phrase of Dylan's scrawled in large black print on the wall: *Fireworks or shooting stars?* I walked closer and kneeled over her. She clutched her journal to her chest. Mascara was caked on her cheeks. Her face was pale. Her hair sweaty on her forehead.

"You look like a corpse," I said.

"I fucked two producers in a row for a record deal," she said. "And now I don't want it anymore."

I tried to draw Laura up, hug her.

"Actually, I fucked them at the same time, one in the ass, one in the mouth. Guess it's a game they play."

"Protection?" I said. "What about Dylan?"

"Oh, Dylan the lady-killer." Laura lit a cigarette and held up her journal. "You know when he found us out there, his girlfriend had just died. She climbed up the fucking roof because he kicked her out in the cold and tried to get in through the chute and fell, fell, fell. Look in there; I found the article about it. Found a pic of her too. Fucking birds in the wild wood."

I turned to the last page of the journal and opened. "But that's you," I said, and turned the photo over. It read: *Danielle, '97.*

"But it's not," she said and stubbed the cigarette out on his floor.

I drew her up, and we climbed into bed. She asked me to hold her heart. "Hold it down," she said. "It feels like it is going to burst." I wrapped myself around her. I placed my hand on her chest until I felt her heart slow. The blue light of predawn smothered the room. I felt the depressions of her scar and imagined the craters on the moon, the craters in the desert.

"Everything here, all these instruments. I hate it," she said. "They were all hers."

"Laura, we just need sleep," I said.

"Can I read you something? I wrote it tonight."

"Shall I hum for you?"

"Yes, you be the music." She began to read. "Everything is winter in summer. August in February. If there is a dream world more true than the waking world, it is us, naked and roaming the desert, modern-day prophets haunted by what's buried beneath us—the ancient oceans, the ancient bones, the ancient names. I had a dream of God. He came to hear me play. I was singing to Him, but my voice wouldn't sound. He froze my fingers. And then snow began to fall, inside the bar and throughout the city, and I knew it was falling everywhere, even over the desert."

Laura started drinking more heavily. Her night with the producers got her a studio date, but the date came, and she called to say she had a chest infection. Daily she announced a new bizarre affliction. I found her in bed at four in the afternoon, nightmares spelled out on her face, her eyes open though she was asleep.

One night I came in through the alley and found Laura screaming at Dylan in the lot, demanding he tell her about Danielle. He held her shoulders and put his hand over her mouth as if hearing the very name was a violent act. When he saw me, he pushed her toward me. She was our child, and now it was my turn to watch her.

"I'm losing my power, I'm losing my power," she whispered. "Please help me."

The next morning, I was late and ran down the subway stairs for the coming train, running with everyone else, running as if from a flood. The stairs were icy from the previous day's snow, late for the season, and in that part of the city, unsalted. I slipped, I landed wrong. My meniscus tore. The doctor said we'd know if I'd dance again in six months. "I don't have six months," I said.

Things changed after I fell. I couldn't wait tables because of the strain on my knee, so I took a job at an office as a secretary. This lack of movement for eight hours a day, shuffling papers, the phone ringing, a blaring computer screen, depressed me as it depresses everyone.

The downers I was prescribed felt good. I had held things so tightly for so long. I had held everything so tight, so tight, I'd fall only to fever. I had held the world inside my chest or else be attacked by visions of its doom. I'd never panted. I'd never stomped the ground. I'd never left my stomach unclenched. I'd never left my hair down from a bun without blow-drying it. I'd never let go of anything.

When Laura drank, I drank with her. She stopped practicing. I stopped dancing. All she did was search for evidence of Danielle. She heaped pieces of clothing she dug out of the closet into a corner of the loft, daring Dylan to rid her of them. In response to this, Dylan stayed in his truck with various women, a different one every night. And Danielle's instruments remained everywhere, untouched.

My father called me back at last after my injury. "I have the sciatica, Ahlam," he said. "It is not so serious. It just means I have trouble walking. You see, I am with you even in this."

"That doesn't really make me feel better," I said.

"I told you not to quit the piano. Isn't there a piano near you?"

"I've forgotten how to play."

"Well, all you can ever do is fight, fight, fight," he said. "That's all we know how to do in this family. Survive."

———

"DO YOU REMEMBER WOODY?" my father asks.

"No, I don't remember any Woody," I say.

"He is the one who saved us in the Superstitions. I picked him up from this hospital in the cab and thought, I know this American guy. I know him. He was sick. He had some disease with the liver."

"I remember now."

"He sang to me in the cab. He was singing. Just like your friend, that Laura. Very nice voice. He sang some song. Moon something, moon child. He's probably dead by now."

"I remember his gun," I say.

"Get me out of here, Ahlam. They're trying to kill me," he says.

The underworld could be everywhere. There were those who wandered into the Superstition Mountains, where my father and I once were lost. With a hunger for gold, they wandered looking for secret mines and were found beheaded. The skeletons of wanderer after wanderer were found in isolated passes of the mountains, their skulls found elsewhere. In the ruined Gowanus Canal, there were rumored to be hundreds of corpses tossed and hidden forever in its depths. Beneath this earth, I once believed there was a basement filled with spirits of those passed. But I know now they are never above or below. We are surrounded.

DYLAN BROKE ONLY ONCE in front of me. He had such a hard demeanor and caved toward upset and warmth only rarely. But when he did, one was compelled to the belief that maybe in fact, he was good. Like seeing the sun after so many cold months. The sun could be so bright, so intense. Perhaps he took cover in endless women, drugs, alcohol, because his pain was more passionate than ours. Because he wasn't just a normal person. He was special. He was starlight. How can we ever believe anything else? The people we've lived beside, the people we've loved. There must be good, we will wait to find it. We must find it.

I found Dylan pacing in the yard, his face red, his boots crunching the glass. "I bought her a bird," he said. "A blue finch."

"How kind." I snorted.

"What was I supposed to do?" He cornered me by the truck, and for the first time I feared him, his height towering over me, his impassive marble eyes. "You two were children. Tell you my girlfriend fell off a roof, and I held her as she died, and I regret the night, and I wish I could take it all fucking back. I wish I had a do-over, but I don't. Now I'm watching it happen all over again like some curse. This is why I keep Laura far. I don't want anyone close to me. Do you think I want this to happen again?"

"We should move," I said.

"You aren't going to go anywhere." He grabbed my wrist hard. "Where else are you going to pay no rent in this city?"

Laura came into the yard. "Calling her Ofelia," she said and walked casually toward us, swinging the birdcage. She leaned up to kiss Dylan. "Thank you, my love." Dylan was crying.

Most of the time, the loft was so full, there was no space for confrontations. Laura would stay in the truck waiting to be loved or banished back to my bed, depending on Dylan's company, his mood. It was always so full of voices of those hoping for another party, another cocktail to drink, the possibility of a night that'd bring them home too late. And Dylan would guide them there. He could guide anyone to the point of no return. He'd corral them with poetry, music, invoking the alcoholic gods that all died young. But we were so young, we didn't know we had anything we would miss.

When Dylan was gone, we took to our corners, Laura humming beside her bird's songs, me practicing my pointe, stretching, anything to hold on to my body. With Ofelia,

Laura sat on the ledge of the window, watching the train snake past, smoking. Then she would sit at the piano. There was music for a few minutes, coming in spurts out of her like a weary machine. The hour she began drinking crept steadily up until it was standard to see her with a tallboy of cheap beer in place of breakfast. By nightfall, there was nothing for her to do but call a dealer to keep her steady, awake, alert. "Let's call in the troops," Laura said.

There were days we barely left the loft. An outing to the bodega was enough, as if we were being kept, propelled back to Dylan's home, as if it were a vortex beyond which we were not allowed free roam.

I slowly lost any dream for myself. No one warned me of this, that the stars in New York can infect the light inside, that they can trap you in their shadow. Dylan was of course a star. He had achieved the thing we all came to New York wanting.

No one had told me that you can wake up, years passed, and not understand the person you are, the things you did the night before, the things you said, the things left undone, that it can feel like a nightmare, a wildly seductive, spinning nightmare.

One morning, I found Laura sitting at the window, twitching. "I've figured it out. New York is too loud to make music in."

"Or it's Dylan," I said.

"It's the ghost of Danielle," she said. "I'm being haunted by her."

"Maybe you have to talk about that night with the producers."

"Maybe you have to talk about why you won't fuck anyone at all," she said.

The sole aspect Dylan was unquestionably generous in was money. He left Laura cash every time he left the house. And with it, Laura began to do cocaine once a week, then twice, then every day, all day. And with ever-decreasing hesitance, I joined her. We sat together in the bed or at the kitchen with Dylan's blades, a picture frame, a compact mirror, sometimes with straws, sometimes with bills, sometimes keys, and together consumed the pale glory.

On the train to work, sleepless, I'd hear women shrieking, coyotes howling in the screech of the subway turns. I'd see rats crowding at my feet and leap into the street only to discover floating black bodega bags. It seemed that every time I was on the subway, a man would stand from nowhere, pacing the car, and claim that he was suddenly moved by the Holy Spirit. "There is someone here on this very train who does not believe in the Savior. And I've been called to stand. I've been moved by my faith to save that damned soul."

Once at work, I'd have to run to the bathroom and splash my face for thirty seconds to stop it, stop the attacks. This was coming down.

But when I was up, I was feverish without fear, in love, my body passionate and full of stars. Higher than any leap could bring me, any rush of performance. I was in love with the world, with the horniness, the meanness, the grandeur of the city crawling beneath my skin. I saw nothing ugly. I saw no war, no calamity, no death, no epidemic, no sudden devil on the train, no sudden devil in my reflection. I saw my body in a wind thick with mint. And I owned every single step.

In Arizona, I drank because I could hear them coming for me, the coyotes howling beneath the floorboards of our new malls and our new schools. In New York, I drank because the night was too short, and the voices of the dead still came for me from the cemeteries landlocked beneath highways and next to airports, from the mighty graveyard across the river blowing dust over us, all of us. In New York, I drank because inside our empty apartments where we lived alone, always alone even if with others, I heard long-dead addicts saying my name, softly and then louder. In New York, I drank to join them. I joined them because they made the voices I heard in my head shut the fuck up. Finally my mind, the things that made me black and blue and blind and ravenous all came to a halt. The blond boy streaked blue and the long-gone Eli and the sadness of my father and the muted desperation of my mother and the eternal return of history and the desert, the shrieking wail of it, the planes' horrible sound, all the sirens, and the flight of dance and the falling down wrong and loving Laura, and wanting to save

Laura, and finding no one in that great big city that embodied it as Dylan, so searing, so empty, all became crossed out, even if a night at a time. In New York, I drank because I was so young it felt like a beautiful thing to let my dreams fall down, and so I shattered them, shattered them good.

The last snow of that long winter, I found Laura beside the canal. She was wearing her mother's fur, its lining undone, hanging forth. Her tights were ripped.

"Aren't you cold out here?" I said.

"Look, Ariel, look. An owl just flew past."

"It's just snow," I said.

"I think the owl is yours, Ariel. I think the owl is your animal." Laura was peaceful. An ambulance bawled in the avenue. Her face darkened in its wake.

"You want to know how my mother died?" she asked from nowhere, looking at the canal and not at me. She had begun to do this more and more. We were losing the ability to look at each other.

"You want to know how she died," Laura said again, gritting her teeth from the high. "She fell. She slipped, and she fell. It's all so simple." She began to laugh.

"I don't get it," I said.

"They think she was running from something," Laura turned to me, her eyes bloodshot, yellowed, starving. "But she slipped. Into the canal. And the current . . ."

As Laura fell silent, I saw them gathering toward us, the

coyotes, their slivers of silver marring the dark, as the five A.M. blue rose over the glittering city—they came closer and closer and closer, so close, I smelled their saliva, their fur, so close I knew by heart their ravenous vendetta when Laura took my finger, with its ancient prick, and pressed it to her own.

APRIL

I WALK OUT OF the hospital and into the wash with a cup of coffee. The sun is bright, so bright that my eyes begin to tear. The sky is marked with wisps of cloud. There is shade only beneath the olive tree, its black juice smeared in the dust. I break off pieces of a creosote bush. I smell the leaves and what little rain is left in them, the purity of the plant's smoke. I smell the leaves and remember my father crushing them in his hands, smelling and sighing, his fingers stained, telling me this is what smells so beautiful when it rains in the desert.

———

I PREFERRED NEW YORK under rain. It made winter days warmer and summer days cooler. It made the spring sad and the autumn sad in the exact same way. Like its sound, it leveled seasons. The years smashed together in New York. Sometimes

I cannot locate any one night as if my life in New York were but a flood of nights. An eternal room full of empty wine bottles, ashtrays overflowing, the maze of screeching trains, Laura at the window, Dylan and his parties, filled with fur and cocaine and moderate celebrity, and the cab rides home, the drunken swipes of credit cards with fifteen-dollar balances behind drivers whose faces I never remembered come morning, dinners with Laura alone, Thai food, not finishing our plates, ordering more to drink, someone at the piano, someone holding the guitar, strumming chords, singing songs, concerts in the beginning, neon flashing, rich acquaintances in Soho lofts, next stop Williamsburg, living in the dark, living in the night, making it through the day only to afford the night. The new trains arrived from nowhere, their sound on the tracks so clean compared to the old, their automated voices, their fluorescent lights, their machines that told us where we were going but not from where we had come as stops, once passed, disappeared from the monitors. How Dylan's place suddenly had a name outside its owner, and therefore was no longer ours but everyone's, less a home than a social event: 979 after its address, 97 Ninth Street.

And then a night comes forward, a night memory won't allow me to forget—the night on which Laura, outraged by her progressive madness, walked slowly down the steps from our home and in her arms, holding a chandelier, a sculpture, as Dylan came to call them, and like an offering walked to the canal, and though we both shouted, Dylan and I, "What the fuck are you doing?" threw it in, and as if we were all under a spell, watched it explode before hitting the putrid water, shatter in blue light. And watching those pieces shatter perfectly, my knee began to hurt like a phantom limb, a phantom wound, for no reason at all. I was no dancer. I was nobody.

We had both gone, Laura and I, as far as we could go, and it was nearly to the end.

In all the years we lived together, Dylan made one meal. Laura slept through it. Burned scrambled eggs with burned bacon. The smell of the fried yolk made me retch. He hardly ate, and that morning was the same. He picked at his food, swallowing a bite every five minutes. He lit a cigarette and smoked over the food. "Do you wish I'd never met you two?"

"We thought we were special," I said. "Meeting you."

"Everyone wants to be special," Dylan said curtly, piecing the fat from the meat of the bacon.

"But we're not," I said.

"But you are." He handed me his cigarette and made himself a screwdriver, shaking the orange juice. "We fallen angels are always mightily tested."

"Sounds like a good phrase for your wall," I said.

"Indeed," he said and began spray-painting his sudden brilliance. "You know what I wanted when I came here? I wanted to build a boat in the yard. I wanted to sail around the world. That's all I've ever really wanted. To never come home to anywhere. To always be out on the water. But I never did. I got caught by New York. Lost in it."

"We're lost too."

"We wait for someone to activate the darkness inside us so we can come into the light. Like moths in their cocoons. Poor devils beside butterflies. Like fucking babies squirted through the womb. Every one of us should carry warning labels like on CDs. You can't blame me. I can't blame you. Nature and nurture. Even the scientists know that. In the end, we make silk. We go to Montauk. We escape the privation of the clock."

WHEN I RETURN, MY father looks drugged. His eyes are watery. He's lost focus. He does not notice the doctor. "You know there is an Indian tribe that believes that on Judgment Day you are held accountable for your conduct in your dreams equal to your conduct in your waking life?" he asks.

The doctor asks for my mother and me to step outside.

"I won't listen to anything you say," my father says. He is singing, a song without lyrics, and then over and over again a chorus he's made up: "Moon child, moon child, moon shine, moon night."

"His temperature has risen a bit. We want to keep him here just to make sure, you know, everything is steady," the doctor says. "He may be having slight hallucinations."

LAURA STILL HAD A way with men. She had a way of never paying for anything. She'd had that way since we were girls when she shoplifted makeup from the mall. One night we met two tourists at a bar. One was beautiful, one was not. Laura tapped one on the shoulder as if she'd known him for years and asked, "Why are you taking so long with our drinks?"

The men looked confused, and then Laura began to laugh, and they laughed back with new desire. We squeezed into the seats beside them, repeating everything twice so they might understand us. They were German. Laura chose the most expensive martinis on the menu, then turned to me. "Dylan fucked you yet?"

"You're crazy," I said.

"He's had the entire city," she said.

I looked at her face in a way I hadn't in years. We stop knowing the faces of those we love, those we see every day, just the way we stop knowing our own. The faces we know day in and day out become automatic, like turning on the ignition, lighting a cigarette. Despite the way she had grown thinner, her hair parched, her face worn, her eyes were still beautiful, magnanimous, unavoidable. They had grown lighter, their amber more brilliant. The rings beneath them were now grey and deep, but they broadcast such impossible innocence. Sometimes she would appear naked before me, undressing on the way to the shower, and though she had paled from our days in the desert, her body still glowed in contrast to the stark loft. Her small breasts cast perfect shadows on her skin, her funny walk, the way her ass seemed to speak, sashaying with sweet attitude so opposite to her swan neck, so elegant, regal. She was a thing so alive, always. She couldn't not be looked at.

She got up to go to the bathroom. When she returned, a dust of white powder was crusted above her lip. "The curse is back!" she said to the men.

I licked my finger and wiped her nose.

"Don't be a hypocrite," she said.

We stayed with the Germans until two in the morning. In the end, while they were outside smoking, Laura stole their change from the bill they had footed for us. The bartender grabbed her wrist. I threw my half-full glass at him so he'd release her. It hit his shoulder. We ran for blocks, the bouncer chasing after us. We ran as if in a dream. The streets were dark. I slipped at one point, and Laura pulled me up, then hailed a cab.

"Let's get high," Laura said when we were safely inside the car. She said it as if it she were saying, *Let's swing, let's jump on the trampoline, let's run through the sprinklers.* She said it like a child. "Wasn't that so much fun?"

Our entire friendship was in the back of that cab we took at fifteen, the Superstition Mountains disappearing behind us, the windows rolled down, the dawn rolling up, the wind in our hair, going home together far too late in silence.

Years passed in New York. They passed quickly. There were beautiful nights running home in the rain, standing at the canal and watching it snow. There were the rare sober nights spent in movie theaters crying at foreign films. There were the nights Laura and I danced in bars alone far past four A.M. The shutters closed, a secret crew smoking and laughing and defying the morning. There were Saturdays on rooftops when someone played a song we had not heard since we were kids, and we were thrilled. The world still might be ours. There were the few parties, where perhaps we met someone who gave us the impression that they believed in us, that they would help us in some undefinable but essential way, through whiskey eyes. But Sunday always came. And with every Sunday we were sadder.

The subway was my solace. I memorized the variance in the sound of the trains. The A's low rumble as if it had inherited the knowledge that its journey ended at the ocean. The difference between the new F and the old F even before it pulled into the station. The torturous turns the 2 made as it pulled in and out of Park Place. The tender whirr of the G. I studied the faces of other commuters. I tried to imagine their pain, their bliss. I still stayed on the train past my stop and took it to Coney Island. Sometimes I rode the Ferris wheel alone just to feel the wind, just to see the sea. I loved it in winter most when all that was open was a hot dog stand, the conductors lazily chatting in the train yard about their children, their shifts. Rubbing their arms from the freeze, wearing only their blue knit MTA sweaters. It could have been anywhere in America and in the off-season, it seemed the New

York everyone had received, all glittering, claustrophobic, vertiginous, was completely elsewhere.

Everywhere we went, everyone was on drugs in a frivolous way. We believed we were too, but we were on drugs in a heavy way. It was such sordid glory, to be the one always with the number, always with the secret bag tucked in our jeans, in the foil of our cigarette packs, in our rundown lipsticks. To be the girls at 979 who knew where the stash was. There were too many people now to simply leave it out on a table. Laura and I had purpose. We were possessed with the power to ensure all the beautiful people wouldn't leave the night without getting high.

In time, though, Laura began to lock herself in the bathroom for hours, talking to herself. She took chairs out to the lot and sat staring into the canal, missing the party entirely. And in time, I was exhausted if not high, a shell of a person. And some nights, alone in my bed, I felt that my heart might cave in at any minute. Some nights I walked home through the snow or the rain or the heat, walked until the dawn fell and saw death. I saw auras, patches of sky vacuumed through. I believed I saw the devil once. He had a bellowing face. He was beautiful. Dark complected, tiger eyed. He was far from me, across the room from me. I could not help but be drawn to him. I began to get closer. I could hear him say as a vial was placed in my hand, "And in the end, even God will have to admit that all those who wandered here wandered toward good."

Dylan was snapping his fingers in front of my face. "Ariel, you want some or what?"

"My bones are sore," I said.

———

I SEE THE PANIC in my mother's eyes. "I have to go out for a while . . . I need some air," she says.

My father's nurse comes to change his sheets. They are entirely wet. I long for a drink. It is not even noon. I can see that the heart rate on his monitor has elevated. His blood pressure too. I can see his soul on that monitor. I remember suddenly to pray. I do not believe the words that run through my mind as I recite silently. But I repeat them beneath my breath, over and over again.

———

THERE IS THE BODY of history ever atop of us, and the body of memory rustling within us. Between the two, we are crushed. At 979, it was eternally 5:13 in the morning. The dawn is so violent when you've stayed up all night. At that hour, I see the three of us at Dylan's table or in the truck, doing lines of whatever pill or powder we could find, downing the last drip of whiskey, so high we screamed at the dawn for its innocence. Some nights in bed alone, I tried to pray. Tried to repeat the words my mother used to hush me up in my childhood bed. *Shema Yisrael.* But the rest of the words wouldn't come. I hadn't prayed since fifteen. That night long gone, sitting in the backseat of the meth car, behind the blond boy streaked blue, gazing at the desert still as midnight, believing time was not a circle but a ladder that only led upward.

One morning, I looked at the clock and saw that it was 5:13 when Laura begged me to come up on the roof with her. We waved at a train. No one seemed to notice. No one waved back. No one was looking out of the train window at that hour. They were good people. They were going to work.

That night on the roof, Laura said, "Let's jump." She said it over and over again, giddy. *Let's jump, jump, jump.*

I thought of what my parents would be doing at that very moment, asleep together at the end of a long night, my father closing the garage as the blue dawn rose over the desert. His taxi safely inside. Everything slowly gaining color and definition with the song of the birds. "Come on, Laura. Let's go down."

"Maybe if we jump," she said, "we won't fall, we'll just keep going. Didn't you ever play that game as a kid? The Peter Pan game, where you'd fly off some steps and see how long it'd take you to land?"

"Danielle is not Laura," I said. She threw her cigarette toward the tracks, then took both of my hands and began to whirl me around and around and around.

"What does it feel like to have a mother?" she said as we spun.

"I have to stop," I said. Laura sat down cross-legged and

pulled at her hair, waiting for an answer. "To have a mother feels like somehow you are safe."

"Safe," she repeated. "Maybe that's why I'm so unsafe."

"It's five fifteen," I said.

"So?" she said. "Since when do you care what time it is?"

At last I went home. While I was there, my father stayed out wandering in his taxi every night. I'd hear the garage door at three in the morning, his slow shuffle through the door, the clink of ice in a glass.

While he was out in the night still in pursuit of his alien ship, my mother and I would share two bottles of wine and sit before the television. She'd fall asleep halfway through the first movie. I'd shake her awake around midnight, bring her to bed just the way I always did. "How'd you finish all that wine?" she'd say.

Finally my father broke his silence. "Let's go take a walk, Ahlam. Let's go to the reservation." As we walked, he would take a step and wince. We rested every hundred meters. "I just need to go in for another procedure. Just one more this time," he said.

An hour later, we were in the car. I was driving him to the hospital.

"Just down Mountainview, like the way we used to go."

"I know the way, Dad."

"I just need them to give me morphine. It's the only thing that makes the pain go away," he said.

On the drive home, dazed and dreamy, my father spoke. "The one they nearly left in the road out of Palestine . . . that was me. I am Yusef. I am the curse. She nearly left me, my own mother. I brought this tragedy." From his pocket he produced a fifth of vodka.

"Dad, you can't drink with that medicine," I said.

"We are all cursed. We live in the era of the curse. A world that cannot be fixed. The best thing would be an alien ship. Another planet. One with three moons. But you, I saw you in my dreams. I saw you coming. You came to heal my broken heart. That's why I named you Ahlam."

I lit a cigarette. "Go ahead, take a smoke," my father said. "It won't kill you. Only sadness will."

For those I come from, there is nothing more devouring than the feeling of want for home, the feeling of need for home. We are all waiting for a form of transport, a ship, a saucer to carry us out of the too-dark night. For my father's family this was called Palestine, for my mother's, it was "next year in Jerusalem." One branch of my blood comprised of wandering in the desert for forty years at my birth; the other of wandering for two thousand, only to find themselves home in a land continually threatened by war. For those who were here before us it was all the names, all the names slowly being erased, names long since renamed, long since buried.

I inherited this longing. I was addicted to it. And so I was at home with those who wanted and never had enough.

I was at home in the places that could never be. The places found only in dreams.

When I returned to New York, it had already changed. I always wished things could just remain. There was a new café on our block between the loft and the train. There were two girls sitting on a patio table at its front. There was a luxury furniture store opening in a month. The Kentile Floors sign was to be taken down. Every day there were new faces arriving in the city, drugged with dreams. Nothing would stop New York. The watermelon men looked on, tilted their hats with less and less passion, suspecting soon, perhaps, they would be disappeared from their own block. I loved the secret spaces in New York, the vacant spaces. The abandoned buildings of Fort Tilden, sand filling the floors, the abandoned homes in the Navy Yard, their windows broken through by tree branches, the outdoor shuttle train in Crown Heights, moving through the snow and the leaves and the forgotten cigarettes, moving on beside the park suddenly as if through the woods. I loved the abandoned subway stations, rushing past the darkened platforms, the sprawl of graffiti like old letters. Letters left by ghosts.

I was still a secretary. There were new horrors to fear. Every day a dog and a cop passed me in the station. We always saw something, but we never said anything. There were new bombs and new famines and new viruses.

One afternoon, I followed a young dancer out of the train at Lincoln Center, her tresses wrapped up in a perfect bun. Her smell soaked the car, her smell of hairspray, of chalk, of lipstick, of hope. I had no business being there, but I followed her until she disappeared through the glass doors. "Hey," I called after her. She never turned around.

When I got home, Laura was on the bed with a man I'd never seen before. The stranger's hair was white, but his face was young, handsome. There was foil on the table with powder in it. Beside it were two syringes. I never learned his name. "It's pure as shit," Laura said.

I had brought my music box ballerina from Arizona, the one I had had as a child. She was blonde, slender and tall. She danced to "Für Elise" forever, as long as you wound her up. She could have spun and spun just like I was spinning and spinning out of orbit except that I could blame no one for it, not even Laura. And so that night, coming down hard and sad and nauseous, my heart beating too fast, I thought it made sense to let my ballerina go. I spun her up and dropped her in that poisoned canal, Beethoven fading as the wind took her slowly away from me.

I RETURN FROM RETRIEVING my mother when I see two officers rushing down the hall toward my father's room. Their guns bang against their legs, and for a moment I fantasize slipping one out from their holsters, taking hostage of the entire hospital, letting my father go free. There is shouting and commotion, and my nails are pressed into my palms, drawing blood.

My mother looks at me, and we both begin to run after the guards. She falls behind me, whimpering. My father's room is empty, the sheets hanging from the bed, the IVs tethered to nothing.

AT THE LAST PARTY I remember, Laura stripped to her bra and underwear, climbed atop the stove, grabbed Dylan's hair, spit on Dylan's face, told Dylan to light her on fire if he wanted to get rid of her. He picked her up and moved her outside like a bag of trash to deposit outdoors while she struggled, kicking against him. He mouthed *crazy* to the guests, making a circular motion at his temple with his fingers to signify such dispensable madness. I went out after them.

He brushed by me on the way back, nearly knocking me over. "I'm not dealing with this." Laura was perched beside the canal, holding her knees, making herself as small as she could. She was smoking, speaking beneath her breath to herself. There was blood caked on her upper lip. She turned to me.

"Is there a lot of it?" she said.

"Laura," I said. "You're shaking."

"Just like that night at that party where I fucked Dylan the first time, and you . . . when I turned over in bed . . ." She wiped the blood off her face with her palm. "I asked you if there was a lot of it."

"I remember," I said.

"I'm sorry I never really asked you about that night," she said. "I'm sorry I didn't save you. Without you . . ." She paused. "How many years have we been here? Time seems to go so fast now."

"You couldn't have saved me."

"I could have," she said. "Remember how dangerous I used to be?" She walked away from me and climbed over the small wall that separated the lot from the canal. She crouched and urinated into the water.

"You'll never give up on me, right?" She took out a vial and put it to her nose. Her hands were shaking, and she dropped it. The glass and the cocaine fell on the rocks, indistinguishable from the grime of the canal. She leaned down.

"Please don't do that," I said. "Please, Laura." She continued snorting whatever she could find, white or not white, manic for it all.

I walked away from her and wandered back into the party. I drank quickly so as to pass out quicker. The party was full of strangers. They were all mockeries. The party was a stream of faces, fractured sentences on labels, tours, galleries, film festivals, acquisitions, engagements, Dylan navigating through it, his face masked with coke, booze, that demonic New York confidence. He was on the couch smoking with a beautiful girl, another one whose name I'd never know, never remember. I fought the urge to throw something at her, innocent as she was. Her dark and flowering hair, her husky, flowering voice.

Laura began to speak of Jesus suddenly. She spoke of angels. She said her angels had come to forgive her sins. Her skin sagged over her bones. She'd lost her breasts. Some mornings I'd find her in the kitchen, her lips blue. Some mornings her face became so white I thought she'd die right before me. Laura heard voices. She switched languages midsentence.

One morning, I found Laura still awake, pacing the length of the apartment, holding Ofelia in her cage, swinging it back and forth like a pendulum.

"Laura, what's going on?" She kept pacing in a daze, as if I were not there at all. "Laura!" I shouted. Finally I ran toward her. She dropped the cage like she'd seen a ghost. The bird clattered about between the bars, terrified.

"What?" she said.

"I called your name three times. You were in a trance."

"Would you leave me alone? You're the cursed one here. All those guys you fucked, dead. Then we get here and what happens?" She kicked the cage again. "Do you hear me? I want you to leave me the fuck alone."

Dylan left us soon after the night Laura broke his chandelier in the canal. She tiptoed out from the lot with no shoes on, dancing around her own spill of glass. Neither of us ran after her. All else could be tolerated or ignored by Dylan, the voices, the agony, the madness, the drug abuse, but not the destruction of his work. He pulled out a bottle of whiskey. "That's fifty thousand dollars she just destroyed," he said. "The bitch is out. The bitch better not ever come back. And after all I did for her."

Dylan and I began to drink. We finished the bottle and then walked to a bar. One of the new bars in the neighborhood. There was a line outside.

"Where the fuck did all these people come from?" he said. "This shit is all bridge and tunnel now. Fuck this fucking city. We're going to *members only*."

At the bar, Dylan took his hand and placed it in mine. I shifted and let his hand fall. "We're losing her," I said.

I wanted him to touch me again. I felt nauseous for wanting it. The sax and the piano and a DJ were going all at once. We were screaming at each other. He went to the other side of the bar. The room was full of people. Crimson lit. Joyous people. No one needed our names.

I began to dance. I hadn't danced in years. Dylan had never seen me dance. Dylan watched me. His eyes haunted me. They were eyes that you saw later. Eyes that made you feel like you were on camera. Eyes of ambition. He was addictive. He was insolent. He was searing. Laura was right. Dylan was New York.

I was falling in the streets home. My scarf dragged, tripping me. Dylan was holding my wrist hard and fast, pulling me on. Where the canal was, I saw a dark forest. Where the coyotes once were, I saw Cerberus.

When we returned home, Laura was waiting for us. She was lying on the floor in the same position I'd found her in a year or so previous, splayed out on the floor beneath Dylan's chandelier, looking at the ceiling as if at stars.

"Hello," she said calmly.

Dylan took a glass that was on the counter and smashed it in his hand. "You bitch," he screamed. His palm began to bleed.

"I'll make it up to you," she said.

"How will you make it up to me? I want you out of here."

"Come here, Ariel. Come get naked and lie beside me," she said.

"I'm tired, Laura," I said.

"Come help me get my boyfriend back," she said. "The two of us can make it up to you Dylan. We can give you a five-thousand-dollar experience. After all, my best friend is the world's greatest blow job girl."

"Leave me alone," I said.

"Please," she said. "Please, please, please. You know you want to. You've always wanted this. I know. I can see inside your dreams."

In the morning, Dylan was gone. My skirt was hitched above my belly. My underwear was on the floor. Nothing ripped.

The glass had been swept up. The blood from his hand was dried on my breast. There was nothing left of the night for me to stuff into a bag. On my inner thigh, there was a wound. His parting mark, a burn from a cigarette. It was blue and purple and more hideous than any of the three I had done on my own arm all those years ago.

Laura was in the bed watching me as I woke, staring hard and dark with a love or a hate so ferocious I yearned to flee her gaze, that ancient, unavoidable gaze. Laura pushed the blanket down to reveal her naked body, lifting her leg to show me her wound. "Blood sisters," she said.

———

I TAKE OFF FOR the doors, leaving my mother with the doctors and the nurses and the guards. I run toward the reservation. I trip over a dead saguaro and for a minute think it a body. In death, the saguaro's needles abandon it. Its carcass resembles a skeleton. Walking upon one in the desert, it is always at first the mirage of a body left to rot beneath the sun. I remember thinking it would make for such a pretty structure for a chandelier, the saguaro's corpse, but of course it would burn. In death, its water abandons it. It cannot hold the rain.

I don't see my father but hear what I believe is a coyote, a raccoon, rustling just ahead. His low mutter in Arabic reveals him. He is walking rapidly, ducking behind saguaros, his hospital gown coming undone, a sheet of white fluttering in the bare brownness of everything. I scream his name. "Dad, Dad, Dad."

"My ship is waiting," he says. "There's no time left."

"You are walking in the middle of the fucking desert!" I say. "There is no ship."

THE MORNING DYLAN LEFT, the room billowing white, I looked out and saw that it was snowing. He was gone. No wallet, no forgotten sock. A note on the wall that read, *You have until October. Off to Berlin, D.* Like he appeared to us with the Lights, he disappeared, without trace or origin. He was the type of man who reinvents his life once every few years, who rids himself entirely and unapologetically of unwinning elements so that he could go on toward his nebulous goal, amass more broken instruments, more parties, more strangers, more collectors, more buried, broken Lauras. This too was his power. He could disappear from the lives of others at any instant without consequence.

I went out in the snow. I held some in my hand. "I'm so sorry," I said beneath my breath over and over again to no one. To myself. It was so pure, the snow, the purest of all powders, I thought, so pure it must be from elsewhere, from another planet.

Laura walked up behind me as if my sorries conjured her to me. "He's gone," she whispered as if there were someone else who might hear her. Someone else who cared. I left her there and went inside.

"Do you hate me?" she screamed.

I have always had recurring dreams about the apocalypse by water. But in one, it is the sun that has fallen and engulfed the sky. "But we are so far from this," I say to the faceless many around me. "The sun won't even begin to die for millions of years."

"It is flaring," they say, "before its time."

"We were wrong," they say. "We miscalculated. It is turning into a red giant. Soon it will be a supernova. We are nearing the end."

Flakes of the star fall like snow in July. Flakes of the sun fall like fireflies. People are opening their mouths and gulping down the sunflakes like rain. "Tastes like rye," one says.

"No, tastes likes blow," another says.

I swallow a flake. "It tastes like God," I say.

My father had called while I was out in the snow. How he had always sensed when I had fallen into trouble, I never knew. As when he demanded we go to the mountains just to see snow the day after the night with the blue-streaked blond. How he knew just what to say, what prayer to read, how to quiet my fears. We both suffered the same nightmares. We both woke up on the same nights with charley horses rattling our calves. We both knew no bounds to our escapism.

"How are you, my daughter?" he asked.

"The snow just stopped," I said.

"Ahlam, one day you look in the mirror and you see your parents' sadness in your eyes. In New York I liked to watch the snow. It is not fair, how quiet it is, the snow, it is not fair. It is not fair the snow does not fall in the desert. It would make so much sense." I heard the cat's whine, the door slam, the car engine, the garage. "My birthday is coming."

"I want to come home," I said.

The day before I left, Laura and I finally turned the space heaters off. Since Dylan had left, we ate in silence. I went to work, and when I returned, she was still in the tent in the truck, often drunk or asleep. We were an even older, an even more weary couple. Neither of us uttered his name.

For the first time in months, the sun reflected off the canal, beamed into the loft, and woke us up with it. It was suddenly spring. Laura came inside from the truck and demanded we go to the beach. "It's still too cold," I said. She began jumping up and down on the bed. She was even thinner than before, her cheekbones popped out from her skin. I hadn't looked at her in so long. I had become afraid of looking at her at all. I could not accept that I was watching her die.

"Okay," I said. "Let's go."

In her purse, she carried a 750-ml bottle of Yellowtail, a medicine bottle of Oxys she pilfered off a dentist, and tucked between the cash in her wallet, a bag of blow. We took the A train out to its last stop, as we'd done in the beginning and hadn't in years. The beach was still closed. No lifeguards, no police. There were no children. We stayed throughout the day. We drank the wine. We spoke of TP-ing houses at fourteen. We spoke of home. The wind off the water was cold. A fog rolled in. I napped intermittently.

"Take a bump?" she asked, smiling at me. I took a bump from her fist. My brain came alight with tenderness for her. I felt so sorry for everything. I yearned to embrace her, kiss her even, to stay with her, always her, my sister, my friend to the end. It was a story after all, even if a sick one. It was completely ours. She stood up and stripped. "Come in with me," she said.

I shook her off.

"Come in with me," she said again, yanking my arm.

"It's going to freeze us," I said.

Laura stuck out her tongue. Somehow, despite everything, she was still a child. Her face implored me, confused, excitable. She was still the girl running through the desert but on a more polluted course.

"Do you love me?" she asked. And then she dove into the waves. The dusk was complete above us.

I watched her and began to laugh nervously as she swam farther and farther out, the fog half disappearing her. "Aren't you freezing?" I shouted. Suddenly her body wasn't visible, and all I could see was her head ducking in and out of the waves. "Laura!" I screamed.

I entered the ocean, the tide pushing hard against me. My

limbs went numb. The cold shot through my blood and my bones. The voices pounded in my temples. *Come come come come come*. They screamed louder and then whispered. I was sinking. Arms came up from the waves. There were bodies beneath me. I had stepped on them, on their chests and their bellies in an effort to enter the water. I knew their faces. Trevor, the blond streaked blue, Eli. And then more, too many, thousands. The water was all limbs. In the mist, the sky fell into the sea. I was burning inside. I shut my eyes. My chest was on fire. The pain would not last. The pain would not last.

I fought my way back to the beach and screamed for help. My knee began to ache like it hadn't ever. There was nobody, nothing. Suddenly I saw Laura's body rise up. She was standing, her waist above the water. I was hallucinating. She was surely dead.

"A sandbar!" she said, shivering when she came up from the water.

"Laura, you're so cold you're blue."

She wrapped herself in the blanket we had lain on and lit a cigarette. Mascara ran down her face. The constellation on her chest was purple in the cold. I began to cry. She began to hum. "What the fuck are you singing?" I asked.

"You know the song, Sleeping Beauty." Laura scooped up the sand and let it fall through her fingers, surveying the grains as if comprised of distinct, tiny worlds.

"Stop it," I said. "This isn't funny."

She crooned on until her cigarette was gone. The ash in the wind blew around us like hesitant snow. "I want to set you free about something, Ariel. But you have to promise you'll forgive me first."

"Just don't drown yourself again."

"I'm a Jonah."

The ocean had ripped the high from me. I felt nothing but panic, fear. I wanted nothing more than to deaden the static going and going in my mind. "What the fuck is a Jonah?"

"Someone who makes every ship sink wherever they go. Someone who brings bad weather. Someone who is cursed." Laura was picking at her fingernails. "There is something else too. Eli, Señor Guapo, he had really nice-smelling sweat."

I looked at her, perplexed.

"So it's not a big deal you were fucking Dylan. I know it wasn't just the once. Because I screwed Eli in his jeep. A day after you did. You told me it was only math homework, remember? And you thought you were cursed. But it's been me all along."

I left her on the beach, her humming reaching me faintly over the waves, the song she sang at the football game all those years ago beneath the fireworks, the one I couldn't place, the one she always sang, far back as it was in my childhood, "Once Upon a Dream." I wanted to walk faster, to run, far as possible from her, from my entire life, from the first day I ever saw her always just a few steps ahead.

⸺⸺⸺

I CAN HEAR THEM coming, their footsteps rushing toward us. I hear a dog bark, my mother screaming at the doctors, the officers calling my name. I take my father's hand. "I'm coming with you."

"It's just there. Do you see it?" Tears run down his cheeks. His hands are cold with sweat.

"I see it," I say. I walk him in a circle. I walk him back toward the fluorescence, the windowless halls of disinfectant, the heart monitors, sheets and beds and sheets. He stops.

"It's just there," he says again. Something shimmers in the distance. A veil of water. A mirage.

⸺⸺⸺

IN THE MORNING LAURA was by the window with Ofelia. She was smoking a cigarette, looking out as the trains passed. "I was just being crazy. I didn't mean any of that. I was having a little schizo moment, you know. Eli, Guapo, whatever. That didn't happen. But I did mean it about the Jonah thing . . ."

"Maybe the worst part is that it has nothing to do with us," I said. I put my arm around her mildly. "Maybe I'm a Jonah too."

"I'm with you," she said. "You thought you were following me, but I was following you too. Always. Always."

As I walked out of the door, she called after me. "Ariel . . . we live in a world of crippled hearts. But we shall still love. Remember the rain will always follow you. And to listen for the trumpet."

I did not turn around. When I boarded the train, I saw the sight of our little home beside the canal, the canal carved through the abandon like a crucifix.

It was my father's birthday. He wanted to have a picnic by the lake. It was the only body of water for miles. It was man-made and nestled between the mountains. The water was brownish and full of mud. There were no fish, and signs everywhere warned against swimming. But the sight of any blue against the desert rock brought relief.

My father already had trouble standing, and so my mother and I took either side of him as he limped toward the beach. He tossed his head up and down, soaking his hair. "You must touch your head to the water, Ahlam. You must submerge it every time. Remember this when you go to the ocean," he said. "This is how you rid yourself of the evil eye. The salt gets in your hair to your shoulders."

"But there isn't any salt in this water," I said.

"Just pretend," he said.

After his ritual, we ate egg-and-tomato sandwiches under the sun. "Why don't we take a trip to see the real ocean?" my mother asked.

"With what money?" my father said. "It's my birthday, and

I am very happy being here at the lake with these delicious sandwiches."

Night had fallen on the drive home from the lake. "We are from somewhere else," my father said.

"We used to be from somewhere else. Now we are from here. This hellhole," my mother said.

"You and I, your mother, Ahlam, we are from up there," my father continued. "We come from the stunning stars. We were just born in the wrong place. We were meant to live on another planet. The people who come to the desert are those who know this, deep inside of them, we are from up there. From far, far away."

"No one knows how to listen in this family," my mother said. "Don't learn that from your father. Ariel, why aren't you saying anything? You've spoken three words this entire trip."

"Do you really believe in curses?" I said.

"Of course I do. I was born inside a curse," my father said. "Don't you know the story of the Bedouins in the desert who used to dig and dig for water? All they wanted to find in the dirt was water. All they needed was water, but sometimes they found a black liquid instead. And they knew if it was black, not blue, that God had cursed them. That they were being punished. They would wail and scream and plead to not find it ever again. Every time they saw black instead of blue. Well, suddenly the West needed that black liquid. And some of those Bedouins became rich from the very same thing they used to believe was a curse. But oil is still a curse. Would there be war at all if it weren't for oil? How many millions have died for that black liquid curse?"

Sitting in the backseat, gazing out at the few stars in the dark, I thought of all of the nights in New York I'd come close to death, all the nights I pushed it too hard, of the booze and drugs I had consumed to escape my losses, realizing that if I had succeeded, my ghost would yearn to return to the one place I'd tried to flee, the desert, being driven by my parents, fighting in the front seats, being driven through the dark toward home.

I awoke in the middle of the night in my childhood bed, and there were tears on my pillow. I had been crying in my sleep. I had been dreaming of my mother at the Sea of Galilee. Rather than one large semicircular lake, it spread out like a true ocean, with bounded bays and smaller tributaries sprawling up into the land. We dove into one such islet of water, its water grey but clear. Once submerged, we saw that there were women, naked, floating beneath its surface, their hair perfectly intact, women dead since Jesus came.

Laura was there. Her hair was purple. I was consumed with love for her. Her scar was gone, her chest smooth and blank. I swam toward her, but my mother urged me up toward the surface. We had to find my father, she said. We swam and swam and then once again had to go below the surface because dusk had descended and the bombings had begun, so we stayed beneath with the other women, but I could no longer find Laura.

"We need soap," my mother said.

＊＊＊＊

MY MOTHER WALKS TOWARD us. The guards remain on the sidewalk, ready for us. This day has already happened; this day will not end. My father is muttering beneath his breath.

"Tell me the story I told you when you were a child, Ahlam. The Sufi one about the butterflies . . . I forget how it goes. Tell me while we wait."

"Yusef," my mother says.

"You joined us," he says.

"There are three butterflies that dance around a flame. The first butterfly comes close to the flame and says, 'I know all about love. It is beautiful, unforgettable.' The second butterfly wants to get even closer than the first, so it does. But it singes its wings. So it withdraws. Terrified, the butterfly says, 'I know that love only burns.' But the third butterfly doesn't say anything at all. The third butterfly simply throws itself into the flames and is consumed."

The rain has arrived. My mother and I hold my father's hands. I take the leaves of the creosote and put them to my father's nostrils. "Now that's the smell of heaven," he says.

Somewhere a television is on. Somewhere there is talk

of the beheadings, of the air strikes, of the new epidemics replacing the old, of another massacre. The earth spins further from help. Beyond us the heart monitors go on, the fluorescent lights buzz, the commentators shout, the casino leaves fall into the desert, sirens blare. But all we hear is the rain.

⸻

I RETURNED TO NEW York at dawn on a red-eye. I longed for Laura. I had to tell her we would survive. That I forgave her everything. We would survive even ourselves, as long as we were together.

I took a right into our lot. The moon was full over the canal. I galloped through the alley and past the boulder. The sky was blue and satiny, and the city just beyond was softened in it. New York was always so beautiful in the very crux of parting with it. It was finally spring, and the winter that year seemed to never end.

There was music wafting out from the loft, classical music. I thought Laura was playing. I turned the key. Ofelia was squawking loudly, batting against her cage. I saw Laura. The sheath of the piano was open as if just used. A song was on the record player. "Kol Nidre."

"Laura," I said. I walked to the window. I sat on the bed beside her. She was wearing a charcoal-grey dress. Her mascara had dried on her cheeks. There was residue of powder on a book. An empty bottle of wine. The Oxys emptied. A syringe on the floor. "Laura," I whispered. I lay down beside her. The train lights moved above us, refracting off the window. Through my sudden tears, the train lights smeared like shooting stars. Lying before the rippling blue window, below the slurred lights of the world above, it was as if we were underwater. "Laura, you're cold," I said.

VII

OCTOBER

THE JEWISH NEW YEAR fell late this year. It was a day of rain. I did not go to work. I woke up from dreams of snow pouring down, thick and white, breaches of sky laced with stars, purple nebula, the world cooing slow as song, and looked into the grey out the window, and not sick, decided to stay. I called my father and said I was coming home.

On that day of rain, I watched it fall on the city, the buildings shrunk by the clouds. It was prettier that way. Laura's things, my things, had all commingled in a chaos that sprawled the entire loft. Laura's clothing and the broken instruments remained on their bellies. I had no idea what was mine in it any longer. Dylan would return any day, I knew. I had bought all the time I could.

I walked in circles about the apartment, tiptoeing over brooms and coins and bobby pins that once held Laura's hair until my chest began to ache as it had intermittently in the months since she passed. I saw a doctor who told me there was nothing wrong with my heart, that it was likely sympathetic grief pains. I went out to the truck and climbed into that bed for the first time since she died and wondered at how loud the rain fell on the tent. Beneath the pillow was something hard. Laura's journal.

———

SLOWLY WE MAKE OUR way through the reservation back to the sidewalk. A wheelchair awaits my father. The crowd that has gathered is smiling. As if this were some sort of home-coming. As if we really had taken off. But they are smiling because they have won.

"I won't get in that," he says.

"We just need to make sure your fever has gone down," the doctor says.

We walk slowly through the halls, my father slightly leaning into my mother and me. "No pain, no pain, no pain," he says over and over again. "When we leave, if I have to fill something out like 'country of birth' . . . I will say I do not know where I am from. I have no birth certificate. I was born walking. That is what I will say, Rachel. My country disappeared when I was born."

———

AFTER LAURA DIED, SHE appeared in my dreams every night. The dreams were variations on the same theme. In them, we were sitting by the canal at Dylan's. Or we were sitting on the reservation in Arizona. And I'd say to her, "Laura, you are dead. How did you get here?"

And she'd say, "No, I'm not. I'm not dead. You made a mistake. How could you believe that I was dead? I never died." Only once in any of those dreams did we embrace. She hugged me violently, lay on top of me, and put her head to my chest to hear my heart. I pushed her off, fearing mine would stop in her arms. In most of the dreams, there were no hugs. We remained talking, fighting gently or viciously for what seemed like hours, but it was only minutes or perhaps a second, because it was only a dream. Then I got up to go somewhere. I had to get something, though I didn't know what, and when I did, I looked up at the sky, and it was as if it was coming apart at the seams and the spectacular reaches of deep space, the nebula, the indigo star clusters, they were all coming in, coming closer. And when I went back to find her, to tell her to come and look, to tell her I'd found heaven, she was gone.

In Laura's journal, I found nothing I had not already seen. I saw Danielle's photo again and realized how little they looked alike. That it was only the shape of their eyes that bore any resemblance at all. The fact I had thought otherwise for so long seemed like the cruelest trick of Dylan's. That the both of us needed so much to feel we were special, singular, that our being there was intended, that neither of us, in our own ways, was just another dispensable girl.

Tucked into the journal's flap, I found Laura's birth certificate and social security card. Born in February, in Arizona, to the name Sonora Gavin.

I felt her in the truck with me suddenly, as if my reading her name had conjured her back. I knew she was there considering me, saying my name in a language I'd never understand. My shoulders and my forehead were pressed down upon as if by a huge weight, the weight of the dead. There was no escape. I leaped out and, hearing my own footsteps echoed back to me, began to run, as if I were being chased by real feet.

There was a new wine store. It had appeared from nowhere in the last month. The other liquor store we'd frequented all those years, the one with the bulletproof glass as its casing, had shut down. This store was dimly lit, spare. There were bowls of orchids. Sophisticated elevator music played. It might have been a spa. There were pairings written on a board in chalk, not pairings for food but for moods.

The girl at the register complimented my bracelet ensemble. I hadn't spoken to a living person in two days. I let her give me suggestions. I let her talk at me. "This one is dry and bold and very complex," she said. "A great year too." I imagined the wine staining my lips.

On the way home, on the bridge of the canal, three young Orthodox boys approached me. "Are you Jewish?" they asked.

"In a way," I said.

"Well, that counts. Have you listened to the shofar today?" the youngest said. I shook my head. "Would you like to?"

"I guess," I said.

"You have to repeat this prayer after me. Do you speak Hebrew?"

"No."

"You just have to repeat after me. Can you do that?" he asked.

I set the wine between my feet. I tossed my cigarette, and we read. Then he drew up his instrument. The sound echoed the wet in the street. People stopped and stared. There was the canal at our side. The city in the distance. The sea elsewhere, the smell of it suddenly close. Here was the trumpet Laura told me to listen for.

"The sounds of the shofar emulate the sound of a cry, every variation of sobbing," he said once finished.

"That's what the shofar is supposed to be?"

"Yes," the youngest said. "And the last, did you hear how it cuts like a gasp, like a pant? It's the last sobs of a desperate man hoping for another year. Shana Tova."

"And to you," I said.

We parted and once over the canal, the drawbridge alarm sounded. The horn of a boat announced its arrival in New York. For a moment the past returned, the canal was a bustling place, a portal scrawled with industry, a place where no one could ever be alone. Once home, I opened the wine and poured it into two separate glasses. One I drank, and one I left full just beside me. *And to you.*

———

"I'M FINE," MY FATHER says. "I cured myself by walking."

The doctor excuses us out of the room, and my mother and I sit again in the waiting room.

"If they let him go, where should we eat dinner?" I ask.

"I can't think about food," my mother says.

"Galileo?"

"It's been gone for years. It closed before you left," she says. "Don't you remember?"

"What happened to that waiter? Tomás?"

My mother shakes her head. "God knows."

———

I DREADED THE COMING autumn. I dreaded the snow that would fall when it was finished. The doctor who told me there was nothing wrong with my heart, told me I should exercise, and so I walked in circles about the neighborhood as I once did, passing the woman who mooned and screamed at passersby, the woman long gone or dead, and now passing crowds of people my own age coming to the new flea market that had opened, emerging with furs and antiques and old books and artisanal ice cream.

There were nights the pain in my chest became so bad I thought it would be easier to give in and let go. There were nights I could not catch a breath. I meditated on my childhood, vague and distant before high school, where Laura still flickered only on the edge of things.

I thought of my father, in the washes with a stepladder to pick his olives, on his tiptoes to reach the healthiest branches. "Take what's whole, what looks the most alive," he'd said. Once home he poured the olives into vats and filled them with water, vinegar, salt. The olives marinated for a month, sometimes two. They were always bitter, my father's olives. We always said they were the best olives we'd ever tasted.

I remembered the nights we all drove out past the city lights and parked the car with our telescope. We found the craters on the moon. We spotted Mars. "Look up when you are scared. Always look up," my father said. "We've named the night after ourselves. Ahlam, dreams are daughters of the night. Dreams travel to the land of the dead and come back again."

I thought of my mother braiding my hair before dance recitals, placing each strand carefully in a bun. Helping me apply the rouge and the lipstick, and the feel of her hands, assuring me everything was going to be okay. I thought of the hot chocolate she brewed for me every single morning I ever slept at home.

I thought of Tomás on the patio at Galileo, hearing the cars swish beneath us. Tomás drew star maps on the paper tablecloths. The first night we ate there, he drew a picture of the galaxy and pointed to where we were, far from the center. "We live in a nowhere suburb in a pretty mediocre galaxy," he explained. "I don't think I'm from this galaxy at all. I believe I came from the Andromeda galaxy, not so far, but far enough. Maybe that's why I'm an outcast." He drew the spiral of

Andromeda close to the Milky Way, almost touching. Then he pointed to Andromeda in the night sky above us.

"Maybe that's where I'm from too," my father said. We could still see the stars.

But the walking in circles never quieted anything, and one morning I realized the only thing left for me was to run hard and fast. My heart aching, sleepless, just past dawn, the light still blue and red and cold, I set off and over the bridge of the canal and over the bridge into the city and back until the sweat and tears burned my eyes, until there was no difference between them, until my heart beat so hard against my chest, I knew I was alive, still alive, undeniably alive. My limbs, my knees, my lungs all hurt, and yet I could go on, I knew, if I had to. I would go on.

When I reached the corner, the father at the watermelon stand called to me. "Why don't you sit down for a second? Have some melon? It'll cool you down."

"Thank you," I said.

"I've been waiting to have a chat with you," he said. "All these years . . . but now that you're all alone."

"Dylan will be back soon," I said.

"I'm sorry about your pretty friend," he said. "Laura, was it?"

"I'm Ahlam," I said and shook his hand. I hadn't said my birth name in years. "Yes, Laura."

"I'm Daniel," he said. "I lost a lot of my friends in the

war. But running was my therapy. I'd run to Central Park, I'd run all the way to Harlem, if you can believe that. I was a very handsome man. Now, you see, it's hard for me to get to that tree. I fell through a subway grate years ago. I was near gone for this world. But now if I walk to the tree and back, it's enough. It's a miracle. If only they'd get me my money."

"How long have you been waiting for it?" I said. "The money?"

"Oh, years. This city . . ." He sighed. "But it will come. I'll be sure of that. For now, I can get to the tree and get back. And the doctors told me I'd never walk again. You can do anything in this life, I tell you. All of life is alchemy. You own the magic of your path."

THE RAIN FINISHES. THE doctor greets us. "Unbelievable, the fever is gone," he says. My mother begins to cry. "He can go after we get through some paperwork. But I want him to return for a psych eval." We nod. We say we understand. The nurse rolls my father out of the room in a wheelchair. My father winks dramatically, as if all of this, the entire night, had been one great joke.

ONLY TOWARD THE END did Laura and I discover Greenwood Cemetery. We were always in search of the desert: empty beaches, Greenwood, Gowanus. When we climbed the highest hill, she said, "This is the highest point in Brooklyn. We'd have to come here if there was a flood."

I still see us sitting there, hiding from the tourists and the cars, our lives, the bars, feigning to be invisible, a land quiet as the desert, looking out over the rivers that close in on New York, the Statue of Liberty lonely in her centuries-old thrust into the clouds. We are there when suddenly the water begins to rise without warning, and the bridges crumble beyond us and the great city and all those gone from our desert are floating there, a great gathering beneath the waves.

When we visited Greenwood, it was fall. We trampled through the red and yellow patches of dried leaves. We spied from a distance as two gravediggers presided over the lowering of a casket. We were the only attendees of that funeral. But then a man and woman approached us. They had backpacks on. They passed right beside us without acknowledging our presence. A foot closer, and they would have walked through us.

"Which of us is alive and which of us dead?" Laura asked.

"We're dead," I joked. We sat at the base of a tree and shared a joint. Laura laughed and lay her head on my shoulder. Her face hurt, her cheekbones. I noticed she had grey in her hair.

"Don't they say all the memories of your life flood through you when you die?" she said. "That didn't happen to us."

"No," I said.

"What's your first memory?" she asked.

"Being in the woods. A woman brought me a small white pony to ride. White as a unicorn. I was with my parents. And

I began to cry, not understanding why I would be asked to do such a thing. I felt like it was really evil."

"You thought that was evil?" Laura laughed.

"What's yours?"

"The moan of the coyotes in the desert," she said.

Laura's father came to New York the day after I found her dead. He wore a sombrero on his head. He had lost his hair. His hands shook from Parkinson's. He visited the morgue, had the autopsy performed, and then had Laura cremated. I waited for him outside of the crematorium, on a block across the street from Greenwood Cemetery. "I'll take her home with me," he said.

He cradled the urn as if it were a baby, tears in his eyes. "In a few months, I'd like to take her to the sea. I hope you will come. You were such a good friend, like a sister."

"I failed," I said.

"She took after her mother, she always took after her mother," he said. "I tried to love them both, protect them. I'm the one who failed."

We stood outside of the funeral parlor looking on into the hills of graves. He hummed something, a sad melody. Just like Laura.

"Shall we say a prayer for her soul?" he said.

My father taught me to pray in one way and my mother in another. My father led me outside before our walks through the desert, those long walks trailing Laura and her father. "Get down on your knees," he said. "Repeat after me."

"Now look to your right and say, 'Good morning, good angel.'"

"Good morning, good angel," I said.

"Now look to your left and say, 'Goodbye, bad angel.'"

"Go away, bad angel."

"Good morning, Wednesday!"

"Morning, Wednesday."

"Goodbye, Tuesday."

"Goodbye, Tuesday."

"Now what's tomorrow?"

"Thursday."

"And the day after tomorrow?"

"Friday."

"Yes, it will be happy, happy Friday!"

Sometimes for no reason at all, he'd begin to cry.

The bad angels were the jinn, and the good angels were the jinn too, and we spoke to them both in the desert. In Arabic, jinn has the same root as the word for paradise, *jenna*. The word for jinn and the word for paradise both have the same root as the word for madness, *junun*. To be close to the jinn is to be close to madness, is to be even closer to paradise.

My mother prayed every night, though I never heard her speak of God, and though she always thought I was already asleep, *Shama Yisrael Adonai Eloheinu Adonoi E-had*, her hands caressing my hair. She kissed the mezuzah upon returning to our home at night, but never upon leaving in the morning.

I too have developed this habit, of speaking to my angels, to my demons, to Laura, to all those I miss, deep in the night. Never in the morning. The morning is for forgetting; the morning is for forgetfulness.

When I was a child, I prayed differently than them both. I tried to see heaven. And I saw it by night at the sea. Hundreds of bodies, phosphorescent in the moonlight, slow as whales, swimming to a choreography set long before time. Islands here and there, strangers perching amidst other strangers, speaking with those once lost.

No ONE SPEAKS ON the drive down Mountainview Road. The house remains the same as we left it, the same brick, the same peeling tawny paint, but it is somehow smaller than the night before. As if it had shrunk and we had grown unbearably big. There is a television in the living room again. It takes up the entire wall. The cat leaps up and down the walls, his voice hoarse from whining for my father, for us all.

"Hello, you little terrorist," my father says to the cat. He reaches for the remote. I take it away from him. "I can't think right now, I just don't want to think."

"I'll cook something," my mother says.

"No, I'll cook. Ahlam always likes it when I cook," he says.

"I go to Mexico in a week," I say.

"You need to move on," my mother says.

"Isn't this the day of repentance? Remembering? Whatever?"

"Aren't we enough for you?" my father asks.

I walk onto the porch for a cigarette. The moon is a crescent, hanging there, yellow against the dusk, above the only saguaro in the yard. The fountain is on. There is no sound but the water on its fake rocks.

How many times will I watch my father from the corner of my eye, confused in the kitchen, clanking pots and dropping slices of tomato as my mother sweeps in behind him to clean up the juice and wash the plates even before the cooking is done? How many times will I sift through my mother's neatly stacked sweaters, forgetting the sudden cold that comes only in the night, tiptoeing over my father's clothes strewn in disarray all throughout the carpet of their closet? There will never be a time that I won't finger his broken glasses left in the hall or on the bar and not remember every time we sat in a restaurant listening to his complaint of the size of menu font and the dim lights.

I hear the oil crackling and smell the sudden searing of the beef and watch the sun slipping into the earth, the bougainvillea in its last light weeping, the rosebush dead, the cat stalking me with his eyes, and just as quickly as the cigarette has begun, it is over, and my mother is calling "dinner," and we are sitting in the same seats we always have, my father closest to the television, my mother closest to the window, and me between them. We were just like any normal family, sitting down for dinner.

In my last dream of Laura, she was outside my window walking toward the canal. The sky was lit a furious crimson as seen only in the desert. In her left hand she carried a birdcage, its door flapping open. I began knocking on the window violently. Forever passed before a bird flew out. Once it did, hundreds of tiny birds flapped about her, above her. She was watching them, amazed. I could feel them against me, inside my stomach, though I was behind the window. Laura called to me. I heard her voice saying my name from no discernible direction. I began to weep. She waved to me. It was her hands, Laura's hands. Delicate, her nails half painted, half peeled. "You see me how you want to see me," she whispered from just behind me.

I have forgiven Sonora. I have forgiven New York, forsaken the recursion of history. But I do not yet know how to forgive myself.

Long past midnight, after everything that has passed, my father is still awake. My mother is asleep on the couch.

The moon passes between the clouds, puffs them through with light. Faintly, I can hear a coyote moan, far from us, far out on the reservation.

"What are you thinking about so seriously?" my father asks.

"I was thinking about evil," I say.

"Well, that is serious," he says. "But there is no such thing. Some of us choose love, and some of us choose hate. You know the Sufi love Satan. Because they believe he loved God the most, and this was why he would not submit to the lesser creation, Adam. Humans. That Satan was the most loyal follower of God and accepted the greatest separation from Him to prove his love. Truly a fallen angel. There are many ways to see the world, habibti."

"What if we love the black hole in the center of all things? What if we are people like that? People who love to be cursed?" I ask.

"Stop your worrying. Look at the moon. We are in the holy month of Ramadan," my father says and goes to the bar to refill his vodka.

———

It is October. My father says he wants to walk in the sea. My mother says she must see the sea. Laura's father is in Mexico, already, waiting for us.

As we drive, my father speaks for the first time lovingly of New York. "Every Wednesday I walked to Lincoln Center to hear the free music. Walking to Lincoln Center and back to One Hundred and Sixth and Broadway because I did not have enough money to ride the train. And it was all free. Free music. Where do you hear free music anymore? Everyone only cares about money."

"Look, you can see the sea!" my mother says.

In the faces on the street, I look for Maria. In one, I almost see her, but when I look again, it is only a child in a white dress selling Chiclets. We pass the abandoned ship, the ship Laura and I say we'd live on one day, its hull rusted, its paint nearly entirely peeled off. The sun seems in love with the ship, the way its beams pass through its tears and its holes. A magnificently sick ship.

In the evening, we have margaritas and chips and watered-down salsa made for the gringos, and the Mexican singers come and sing "Guantanamera" over and over again. The dock sways beneath us, and in the sea stands one fisherman in his rowboat who joins the singing, and when the singing is finally done, he sits and looks off into the dark ahead. There is no moon. The stars have risen and fallen and given way to a new spread, to the smeared heart of our Milky Way.

"Look at the lonely fisherman," my father says.

"Look at his view," my mother says.

The Andromeda Galaxy is one of the few blue-shifted galaxies in the universe. Instead of being torn away from us by a force far greater than gravity, the fate that commands the red-shifted galaxies, the force that will cause all the lights to one day go out, Andromeda is coming for us at eighty-five miles per second. In four billion years, far after the sun has grown too hot for us to live, it will crash into us, into the Milky Way.

My father, a Palestinian, and my mother, an Israeli, met in a bar in New York. Their encounter was a blue shift. An anomaly. A collision. In the end, I understand, it is only for this we live. All I ever wanted was to love.

ON MY LAST DAY in New York, the sirens would not stop, the helicopters were searching for someone, something overhead, but there was no intercom, no principal that could personalize the calamity around me. I packed my snow globe last. It held the old Manhattan skyline. And I looked out at the view beyond me, of the city, the void of the towers, of the view of New York then, in that little glass ball, and the view of it now. That even in those two visions, there was the coincidence of missing.

One last time, I walked into the bodega, greeted the obese cat, told all the men there whose names I'd never known, men I'd seen every day for years, I was leaving. "We will miss you," the owner said. "Hope they have a good bacon-egg-and-cheese where you are going."

I passed Daniel and his son. They tipped their hats. Watermelon season had ended. "Safe trip now," Daniel said. I thanked him. I said goodbye.

It was still raining in New York. I stood beneath the above-ground awning waiting for the train. I looked out at the canal. The still canal. New York had changed shape already. It had changed its smell. It was already a foreign city to me. I was among strangers. There were five of us there, crowded beneath the tiny awning, waiting for the rain to pass. Waiting for the train to come.

I was intent on holding the scene when a beautiful stranger approached me. "I know you," he said. I didn't remember him. I'd remember such a nice face. "Don't you remember me?" he asked. "It was years ago at a party where we met, but I know I know you."

I faded out. I was for a moment my father tapping on his cigarette, the way he holds it, crushing it flat. I was my mother at the sink, staring into the desert from the kitchen window, dishes in hand. I was in all the beds I'd ever slept in. Me sinking into the sheets, letting my thoughts fall down. I was running alongside the ocean, Laura splashing me with water. I was dancing to a melody I did not recognize, spinning wild and lovely into exalted leaps. I was no one again. I was someone with no name, no past. My face resumed the freshness of birth, the brightness was again in my eyes, the brightness only children own before life begins its wreckage.

The grey light surrounded us. It allowed all other colors, the colors of our jackets and our shoes and our umbrellas their true brilliance. It was not all a dream. This must be my version of awaiting the messiah. Watching the rain, finding cover. "Hello," I said.

———✕———

WE HAVE DRIVEN THROUGH the desert, all the way to its end. The saguaros are replaced by sand dunes. We have arrived at the sea. It is morning. We walk the stretch of the beach, the autumnal wind like May in our hair. My father says he feels no pain, no pain at all. "It's the sea," he says. "It must be the salt air. Maybe the curse has gone." My mother does not cough once.

With us walk a trumpeter, an accordion player, a guitarist, two small girls with tambourines. They play a cheerful song. One made for piña coladas and first love. When they finish, they play it again. Before it is all over, I ask at last why Laura went by another name.

"She hated the desert. She hated it ever since she was a girl. She always wanted to live by the ocean," her father says and walks on.

We follow him to the water. He is wearing a sombrero to shield the sun. We do not exchange a word or a gesture. He climbs a wall of rocks that juts out into the sea. We stand on the sand below him in a triangle. My father prays. The sea rushes up to us. Her father kneels and unclasps the urn. Above the waves she falls graceful as snow, my sister, my Sonora.

We stay through the dusk. The music does not stop. The players gather, depart, walk a stretch to another group of players, and play again. There are children swimming in the sea. The tide stretches farther and farther away from us. I feel a burning spread across my chest and for a moment believe my skin sprouts lightning tracks. I hear Sonora's voice inside me one last time. I think of the stranger in the rain. The one I knew, the one I once met. I wish he could be beside me now, far away as I am. Venus burns hot and bright amid a parade of stars whose names I do not know. A wave rises, lost in the black sky so large it might be a whale, and then breaks long before shore.

This is it. This is how I always saw heaven, always by the sea, always by night, always in the dark.

For book club discussion questions on
Hannah Lillith Assadi's *Sonora*, please visit
bit.ly/SonoraBookClub

ACKNOWLEDGMENTS

MY DEEPEST GRATITUDE IS owed to PJ Mark for his enduring faith, Marya Spence for her invaluable assistance, to Mark Doten for his brilliant vision, and to Meredith Barnes, Rachel Kowal, and everyone at Soho Press—all who tirelessly made this dream real.

To Joe and Anya Stiglitz for their support throughout, for bringing me along on the tour, and to everyone in suite 212 who lent an ear to the struggle.

To early readers: Laina Macrae, Predrag Milovanovic, Andrew Spano, Binnie Kirshenbaum and Robert Lopez for their profound guidance.

To Donald Antrim, Rivka Galchen, Ben Marcus, and long before them Susan Mashburn for their teaching, and to fellow writers for their wisdom in all the workshops over the years.

To Kellam Clark for his dark, magical home on Dean Street.

To Jonathan Thomas for the desert walks in the early stages of this book and to Ben Sandler for all the Starbucks cigs and for Paris.

To Jesse Glendon Tillers for her songs and for all the gorgeous, howling nights.

To Sabra Embury, Maria King, and Ashley Villarreal for their incomparable strength, sisterhood, and inspiration.

To Elena Megalos for living inside this book with me over the years, for her steadfast devotion and loving friendship, without which I would have been lost.

To all those who passed away too soon at Desert Mountain High School, this book is also dedicated to you.

To Gandalf Gavan for so much, but mostly for impressing upon me that I had no choice but to write, and whose life endures on every page of this book.

To my mother, Susan, for living bold and true, for your unconditional love, for being my best friend and advocate, and for believing in an improbable dream.

To my father, Sami, for teaching me how to fight then fight harder and what it means most profoundly to find home. For your heart, your compassion, and your courage. You are the strongest lion I know.

And finally to Jake Gwyn, for leading me out, you are my Orpheus, and for letting me look back from time to time for the sake of this book.